WIFE W

Rich and Hands
who likes kids and pets needs a wife.
She must be pretty and nice and also
like kids and pets.

Deer Prens Charmng, My mama
is nice and prety. Pleas pik her
my dady is dead.

Love, Zach G.

Ruth Jean Dale lives in a Colorado pine forest within shouting distance of Pikes Peak. She is surrounded by two dogs, two cats, one husband, and a passel of grown children and growing grandchildren. A former newspaper reporter and editor, she is living her dream: writing romance novels for Mills & Boon®. As she says with typical understatement, 'It doesn't get any better than this! Everyone should be so lucky.'

Recent titles by the same author:

PARENTS WANTED!

BY
RUTH JEAN DALE

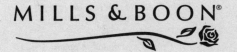

MILLS & BOON®

MILLS & BOON and MILLS & BOON with the Rose Device are registered trademarks of the publisher.

First published in Great Britain 1999
Harlequin Mills & Boon Limited,
Eton House, 18-24 Paradise Road, Richmond, Surrey TW9 1SR

© Betty Lee Duran 1999

ISBN 0 263 81752 0

Set in Times Roman 10½ on 12½ pt.
02-9908-42017 C1

Printed and bound in Spain
by Litografía Rosés, S.A., Barcelona

CHAPTER ONE

Mrs. Forbes, longtime receptionist at the Rawhide, Colorado, *Review,* looked up from her word processor with a smile. "Why Jessica Reynolds!" she exclaimed. "How are you, honey? I haven't seen you since your ninth birthday party and that was at least three months ago!"

Jessica shifted uneasily from one foot to the other, thrusting her hands behind her back so Mrs. Forbes wouldn't see the plastic shopping bag, or be curious about its contents. "My birthday is April sixteenth," she said. "Thank you for the soccer ball."

"My pleasure." The nice lady beamed. "Would you like a jellybean?"

"Yes, thank you." Mrs. Forbes always had a bowl of jellybeans on her desk; you could tell she was a grandma. Jessica scooped out a handful and popped several into her mouth.

Mrs. Forbes nodded approvingly. "So what brings you here to a boring old newspaper office on this fine July day?"

Jessica spoke around a mouthful of candy. "I came to see my grandpa. Is he here?"

"He sure is."

"Can I talk to him?"

"You sure can." Mrs. Forbes pointed to the closed door with the sign that said *Editor, Publisher, Owner and King.* "Go right on in, honey. He's been working on that editorial for two hours already. If it's not right now, it never will be. And you can tell him I said so!" With a final smile she returned to her typing.

Jessica popped the last of the jellybeans into her mouth and squared her shoulders. She had come to see her grandfather on *a very important mission* and she didn't want to make any mistakes. With purposeful steps she marched to his office and threw open the door.

John Reynolds looked up from behind his big desk with surprise on his jolly face. His thick white hair stuck out in all directions and Jessica thought in passing that he needed a haircut. But then, so did her daddy, most of the time. So did she, for that matter.

Grandpa grinned broadly and turned away from the word processor on the corner of his desk. "Hi, there, Sugar. Come give your favorite great-grandpa a big kiss!"

"You're my only grandpa, and you *are* great," Jessica said, because she knew he expected it. She only had one grandpa but this one would be her favorite even if she had ten grandpas. She trotted obediently around the desk and planted a big smack on his cheek, being careful to keep her shopping bag behind her.

He continued to beam at her. "So what brings you to my neck of the woods when you should be out playing with your friends?" He waved her toward a chair beside the desk.

She slipped into it, dangling bare brown legs over the edge of the seat. Maybe she should have dressed up for this important job? Her grandfather seemed to like seeing her in dresses and here she was in old cut-off jeans and a faded red T-shirt. She frowned, suddenly realizing that her sneakers had identical holes over the little toes of both feet. She sighed. Too late to worry about that now.

He was waiting for an answer. She pursed her lips and tried to think how to begin. "Well, see…uh…"

He stopped smiling but he didn't look mean or anything. "Hmm…" He cocked his head to one side. "Looks like you mean business this time, young lady."

"I sure do!" Jessica popped to her feet, finally hauling the bag around in front of her. Placing it on the floor, she reached inside and pulled out her piggy bank, the white ceramic one with the red spots that Grandpa had given her Christmas before last. She placed the bank on the desktop before him.

He leaned back in his chair, hooking his thumbs in his suspenders. "What's this!"

"All the money I have in the world," she said fervently. "I hope it's enough."

"Enough for what?"

Turning, she rummaged around in her shopping bag again and pulled out a folded piece of notebook paper, her heart pounding. Holding her breath, she offered the paper to him.

He unfolded the page and spread it out on the desk with great care. Picking up his glasses, he perched them on his nose and began to read.

Jessica held her breath. She'd put a lot of thought into the advertisement she wanted to place in her grandfather's newspaper. Hadn't he always said you could find anything you wanted, or get rid of anything you *didn't* want, with an ad in the *Review?*

She was about to put him to the test. She'd worked very hard on her ad, copying it over and over, trying to get all the words just right. She'd read it so many times that now she could recite it by heart:

"'Wife Wanted. Rich and handsome Prince Charming who likes kids and pets needs a wife. She must be pretty and nice and also like kids and pets.'"

"Well, well, well." Grandpa removed his glasses and peered at her in surprise. "Prince Charming, huh? Are you talking about anybody we know here?"

Jessica laughed nervously. "You know we are, Grandpa. I'm talking about *Daddy!*"

He nodded, looking very serious. "That's what I thought until I got to that 'rich' part."

"Pretty rich," she hedged. "I heard Mrs. Forbes say he was a great catch one time. Is that the same?"

He rolled his eyes. "Close enough for government work, I guess. But I wouldn't exactly call my grandson a *Prince Charming,* either."

"I had to say something nice or nobody would answer the ad," she argued a little desperately.

He chuckled softly. "Is it that important to you, Sugar? Aren't you happy? Isn't your daddy taking good care of you?"

This was the part she'd dreaded, trying to explain to Grandpa how she felt. "He's...he's awesome as a daddy," she said slowly, "but as a mother…well, as a mother, Grandpa, he…he…"

"Stinks?" he offered helpfully.

She sighed. "Yeah, I guess."

"But I thought he had girlfriends. I mean, doesn't he go out on dates sometimes?"

Now it was Jessica's turn to roll her eyes. "Sure, but not with *mothers*. They're pretty and all, but they just pat me on the head and try to get away as fast as they can." She curled her lip at the memories. "That *Brandee* woman is the worst."

"You mean Brandee Haycox, the banker's daughter?"

Jessica blinked. "I don't know. I just know she doesn't like kids much and she *hates* dogs. When she saw Fluffy the first time, she screamed."

"Honey, Fluffy is a ninety-pound Siberian Husky with silver eyes and fangs like a wolf."

She thrust out her bottom lip stubbornly. "That Brandee woman doesn't like dogs! What kind of person doesn't like dogs?"

"You got me there." He cocked his head and he was no longer smiling. "You don't think…you don't think your father's planning to marry her?"

Hot tears sprang to Jessica's eyes. "I hope not, but he's gotta marry someone. I need a mother! I need someone who knows how to comb my hair without pulling it out by the roots." With one hand she flipped up her long straight hair—straight except for the tangles. "And I want to learn how to cook, and I need someone to sew on my buttons and stuff. Daddy's no good at girl things, Grandpa."

"Never was," he admitted.

"So I just have to *do* something." Looking around, she spied the big metal stapler on his desk. Grabbing it, she raised it high above the plaster pig, ready to shatter it to smithereens so she could offer him every single cent.

"Hold on!" Grandpa caught her hand in midair.

She frowned. "Don't you want to know how much money I have? Maybe I don't have enough."

"You've got plenty." He slipped the stapler from her hand. "I'll trust you for it."

That had been a big worry. She slumped with relief.

He cupped her chin and raised it so he could look into her eyes. "This is really important to you, isn't it, little one?"

She sighed. "It is, Grandpa. I'm growing up. I'm almost ten—"

"Barely nine."

"—and I'm gonna be a teenager soon. Somebody's gotta show me girl stuff or I might goof up."

For a long time, Grandpa sat there with a thoughtful and kind of sad look on his face. Then he suddenly sat up straighter. "Okay, we'll do it," he announced.

She threw herself into his arms, so filled with relief that she could barely talk beyond murmuring over and over again, "Oh, thank you, thank you!"

"Here's how we'll work it. We'll run the ad blind—"

"Ads can't see!"

He laughed. "Blind means we won't say whose ad it is. We'll direct replies to the *Review* at Box 100."

"Okay." She didn't understand exactly what the point was but she didn't much care as long as he would run her ad.

"Then when we get in all the replies—if there are any—we'll tell your daddy what we've done."

"Let's pray," Jessica suggested, under no illusions that her father would be pleased. But as he was always saying to her, she was doing this for his own good whether he realized it or not.

"You got it." Grandpa grimaced. "I don't expect that grandson of mine will be any too happy but by then it'll be too late."

They exchanged conspiratorial glances. Then he said more cheerfully, "Anyway, we'll cross that bridge when we come to it." His big grin flashed again. "You see, Sugar, you're not the only one who'd like to see him settle down with a nice girl."

"Who likes kids and dogs," she reminded him, because that was the most important part.

"Absolutely." He stood up. "Take your pig and run along now. I'll see that the ad gets into today's paper."

"Thanks, Grandpa." She hugged him. "But I want you to keep the pig. Daddy says only deadbeats don't pay their bills."

"Well…I can wait for payment until we see if our scheme works out, I suppose. I'll keep the pig until then."

"Thank you, grandpa. I love you."

"I love you, too, Sugar." He cleared his throat. "So where's your daddy today?"

"He's working on Mrs. Gilliam's house."

"Still?"

"I don't think he'll ever get it right," she said seriously, repeating something she'd heard at home.

"Probably not," Grandpa agreed. "Poor Laura. So *that's* why she said she'd be coming in late today."

Matt Reynolds shoved his cap back on his head, planted fists on hips and glared at Laura Gilliam. The life-styles editor of the Rawhide *Review* had to be the pickiest customer he'd encountered since he started the Reynolds Construction Company years ago.

She stared right back at him with an exasperated expression on her face—admittedly a very pretty face but stubborn. Really really stubborn.

He spoke past gritted teeth. "You realize that if you keep changing the specifications on us, we'll never get your family room finished."

Slender brows rose above velvety brown eyes. Her lips were the pink of roses, although set in a straight and forbidding line at the moment. "Don't patronize me, Matthew Reynolds," she said. "This is the only family room I'll ever be adding to this house and I want it to be *right*."

"Right." She wouldn't know *right* if it walked up and kicked her in the shin. What difference was it going to make when she used it, if the bar was six inches to the right or left? But to put it where she wanted it was going to mean changing the door and that meant the windows would have to be adjusted and the refrigerator shifted—hell.

"I knew you'd understand," she said sweetly.

"Who understands? But if that's what you want—"

"It is," she said quickly. "Thank you very much for your…patience?" Her expression said something else entirely, something along the lines of *you're not going to bully me, you big oaf.* "Now if you'll excuse me, I have to get in to work."

"Sure. Don't let me keep you."

She turned and he found himself admiring the curve of her hips beneath the denim skirt, the slender legs, the bounce of blond hair. When she'd first moved to town three years ago to take the job at the *Review,* he'd thought that maybe they might…

But he'd been badly mistaken. Laura Gilliam might look good but she was stand-offish and guarded her privacy too fiercely. So far as Matt knew, she rarely dated, although she was much admired by the half of the population which was male.

Helluva waste.

She disappeared through the door which temporarily connected the new construction with the rest of the house. He heard her call out, "Abby, I'm going back to work now."

Matt knew that "Abby" was Abby Royce, recent high school graduate who was baby-sitting Laura's six-year-old son, Zach, for the summer. He heard a further mumble of voices and then the slam of the front door, followed by the sound of her car engine.

Zach came skipping around the side of the already-framed room addition. "Hi, Mr. Reynolds," he called out, his expression eager as always. "What cha doin'? Can I help?"

Matt grinned. Laura might be a pain in the neck but Zach was a great kid. A great *fatherless* kid, Matt corrected himself—and it showed. The boy was painfully eager for a man's company.

"I can always use a good helper." He waved Zach up beside him. "I was just hoping someone would come along to drive in a nail for me."

"I can do it!" The earnest, freckled face looked almost ecstatic.

"You know," Matt said slowly, "I kinda think you can."

While Zach pounded away, both hands on the hammer, at a nail already started, Matt felt a curious warmth spreading through him. All little boys needed a man around the house. But considering how obstinate this little boy's mother was, that wasn't going to happen anytime soon.

Poor kid.

Running up the front steps of the *Review,* Laura met her boss's great-granddaughter coming down. Jessica was a real sweetie, unlike her moose of a father.

"Hi, honey," she greeted the girl. "Drop by to see your grandpa?"

The girl stopped short and her blue eyes widened. "Yes, but don't tell," she said quickly.

Peculiar response. "Okay, if you don't want me to," Laura promised. Automatically she reached out to brush back brown hair falling across Jessica's eyes, nearly obscuring her vision. Poor little thing; her hair always looked like a haystack. And it would be so pretty if something were done with it.

The girl looked up with wide eyes. "Does my hair look awful?" she asked anxiously. "I combed it this morning, honest."

"It looks just fine." Laura finished smoothing the bangs out of the way. "Your hair is really very pretty."

"It's awful!" Jessica batted at it. "I wanted to cut it since second grade but Daddy won't let me. He *likes* long hair but it gets in my way all the time."

"Why don't you braid it, or wear a ponytail?" Laura suggested; a reasonable solution, she thought.

Jessica's lower lip thrust out. "Because I don't know how," she muttered.

"Well, for goodness sake, if that's the only problem—!" Grabbing the girl's hand, Laura guided her back up the steps. "Come inside. I can teach you in five minutes."

"Really?"

"Really."

And she did. Then she bought Jessica a can of soda and they spent another half hour talking— "Girl talk," Jessica said smugly.

"That's right," Laura agreed, admiring the long braid swinging neatly between the girl's shoulder blades. "Feel free to drop by any time you need help with your coiffure."

"My what?"

"Coiffure. That's hairdo in French."

"Coiffure." Jessica preened. "I didn't even know I had one!"

Because you don't have a mother, Laura thought, feeling infinitely sorry for the pretty little girl before her. And that father of yours apparently isn't doing anything to help you out, either. You're growing up fast and there's so much a girl needs to learn.

Poor Jessica really needed a woman around the house, but considering how pigheaded her father was, that wasn't going to happen anytime soon.

Poor kid.

"Hi, Daddy."

Matt looked up from the building plans he'd been perusing to see his daughter skipping across Laura's lawn. She looked different and for a moment he didn't realize it was because her hair was in a neat braid instead of hanging free around her face.

She looked nice. He wondered who'd done it for her.

She preened before him, turning her head this way and that. "Like my coiffure?" she inquired coyly.

Zach, playing in the grass with a square of sandpaper, frowned. "What's a cough-your?" he wondered.

Jessica grinned broadly. "A hairdo, silly."

Matt smothered his smile. "So who braided your hair and taught you such a big word?" he teased his daughter.

She pointed to Zach. "His mother!"

Zach clapped his hands together. "Hooray for Mama!" He looked expectantly at Matt.

"Yeah, hooray," Matt responded, less than thrilled with the news. "So where have you been?" he asked Jessica.

"Around." She said it with airy superiority.

"Does your sitter know where you are?"

"I told Mrs. Brown I was going over to the crafts workshop at the school."

"But you didn't?"

Zach stood up. "I'm glad you came to my house, Jessie. Want to play?"

Her gaze shifted from the little boy to her father and back again. "Daddy—"

Zach tugged on her hand. "Jessie, I got a new video. Want to watch it?"

Matt frowned. "Jessica, I asked if you've been to the crafts workshop at school." Even in a town as small and friendly as Rawhide, he didn't like the idea of her wandering around anywhere she chose to go.

She nodded without meeting his gaze. "So now can I go see Zach's video? It's probably some *baby* thing but—"

"It's not a baby thing!" The little boy's face turned red. "It's got a horse and a dog and a cow—"

Matt gave in. "Run along, kids. Jessica, I'll call you when it's time to go."

"Okay."

He watched them hurry away, the little boy putting his hand trustingly in Jessica's. Nice kids, both of them.

But now he had to figure out where to relocate the damned door so he could put this project for the picky Mrs. Gilliam behind him.

But Jessica's hair *did* look good.

Zach's baby-sitter gave the kids an apple and a glass of lemonade each, put in the new video and departed to fold laundry. It only took a couple of minutes for Jessica to decide that, Zach's opinion to the contrary, this *was* a film for little kids.

Zach finally looked around at his fidgeting guest with a frown. "What's the matter?" he asked.

"This movie is boring."

"It's not neither boring!" He clenched his hands.

Jessica gave him a superior glance. "It is to me," she said. "Besides, I'm thinking about something *important.*"

"Important?" Zach swiveled around on his seat on the floor before the television.

Jessica examined her surroundings for lurkers. Then she whispered to Zach, "Can you keep a secret?" She felt as if she'd bust if she didn't tell someone what she'd done.

Zach made a big X on his chest with one forefinger. "Cross my heart and hope to die!"

"Okay, then." She licked her lips and leaned forward. "I'm gonna get a new mother!"

"A new—?" His expression lightened as if he'd just caught on. "You are? Who?"

"Don't know yet. I put an ad in my grandpa's newspaper." She pulled out the newspaper she'd picked up in his yard on the way in, turned to the appropriate page and read her ad proudly.

"My mama is pretty and nice and likes kids and pets," Zach said when she'd finished. Suddenly he frowned, then asked sharply, "Can I get a daddy that way?"

"You mean, put your own ad in the newspaper?" She thought for a few moments. "Well, I don't know but I don't think so. In the first place, you don't have any money to pay for it.''

''I have a whole dollar that the tooth fairy left last week,'' Zach objected hotly.

''That's not near enough.'' Jessica couldn't help thinking what a child he was. ''Besides, a mother is probably easier to find than a father.''

''But I already got a mother!'' He looked on the verge of tears. Just then his big old orange cat, Lucy, crawled onto his lap. He clutched Lucy so hard she let out a resentful yowl before cuddling up to him.

And at that very moment, Jessica suddenly had a really brilliant idea....

''You again?''

Jessica laughed and ran to hug her grandfather. ''Aren't you glad to see me, Grandpa?''

He grinned. ''You know I am.'' He gave her a skeptical look. ''Did you see your ad?''

She nodded eagerly.

''Didn't you like it?''

''I love it!''

''Then...?''

''I've already got an answer!''

He stared at her in astonishment. ''But how? The ad's barely had time to hit the streets.''

''I don't care, I've got an answer! I didn't know what to do with it so I brought it to you.'' She handed him a sheet of paper identical to the one her ad had been written on.

Again, he opened the paper and together they read,

"'Deer Prens Charmng. My mama is nise and prety. Pleas pik her my dady is dead. Love, Zach G.'"

"He's just a·little kid," Jessica explained in her grandfather's ear. "I *told* him how to spell 'prince' but he still goofed it up. And he got confused on 'pretty' and left out a 't'—" She glanced at her grandfather and stopped speaking abruptly.

It almost looked as if Grandpa had tears in his eyes.

CHAPTER TWO

THE next day was Saturday, which wasn't Laura's favorite day to work. But this assignment was special: the announcement of the Citizen of the Year in Rawhide, Colorado. The name of the small city's honored citizen would be announced at the annual potluck picnic in the park, to which the entire community was invited.

That meant old and young alike, so Laura and Zach set off for the park shortly after eleven o'clock. Parking in a field designated for that purpose, Laura hauled out her contribution to the festivities—her famous apple pie. She also carried a tote bag containing a reporter's notebook and a camera. Zach skipped along happily at her side.

The day was balmy and bright, one of those Rocky Mountain highs songwriters immortalized and locals cherished. Well-known because of her association with the newspaper, Laura responded to waves and greetings from almost everyone they passed.

This was one of the things she loved about living here—the friendliness of the people and the neighborliness of the town. Everyone had welcomed her when she'd arrived three years ago to take the job of life-styles editor of the *Review*. She'd been a widow with a three-year-old child, both of them strangers from the big city of Chicago, and both somewhat fragile emotionally.

But the citizens of Rawhide had taken the newcomers to their collective hearts—with a few notable exceptions, one of whom suddenly loomed before her as she rounded the last vehicles parked at the edge of the grassy parkland.

Matthew Reynolds: wouldn't you just know. And beside him was his best buddy, Dylan Cole.

Matt tipped his cap and Dylan tipped his cowboy hat. Both grinned broadly, their attention focused on the pie she carried.

Zach tugged at Matt's hand, his little face beaming. "Hi, Mr. Reynolds. Hi, it's me, Zach!"

Matt grinned down at the boy. "It sure is." He nudged Dylan with his elbow. "You know my helper Zach, don't you, buddy?"

"Yep." Dylan offered a hand to the boy. "How you doin', partner?"

Zach put his little hand in that of the big man grinning at him. "Okay," he said shyly.

Matt patted the boy on the head. "Any chance your mama is carrying one of her famous apple pies for this potluck?"

Zach nodded his head vigorously. "Uh-huh. And she's got another one just like it at home!"

Matt looked shocked. His gaze swung from the boy to the mother. "You holding out on me, Laura?"

She smiled sweetly. "And not for the first time, either." She nudged Zach forward. "Come on, honey, I need to put this pie down and then we'll see if any of your friends are here."

"Okay." The boy gave Matt a last wistful glance before turning away.

That's what came from having Matt bumbling around with her remodeling project, she thought self-righteously, following the boy weaving his way through the crowd. Thank heaven, the job would be finished soon—she devoutly hoped—and then surely Zach would get over this bad case of hero worship.

Please let him get over it!

Matt watched her walk away, wondering how a man was supposed to deal with a woman like that. Hell, she even ironed her jeans, put creases in the damned things! And with those nicely fitting jeans she wore a white silk shirt that clung in all the right places. Denim and silk: a helluva sexy combo for an Ice Queen like Laura Gilliam.

Dylan chuckled softly. "Just what did that mean?" he inquired, jutting his chin after Laura.

"What did what mean?" As if Matt didn't know.

"When you ask if she's holdin' out on you, she says it's not the first time. Something goin' on I don't know about?"

"Hell, no." Matt took off in the same direction she'd disappeared. "What say we go liberate us a couple of cold ones."

"Best idea you've had all day."

Tubs overflowing with cans and bottles of beer and ice stood beneath the shade of cottonwood trees. Off to one side, long trestle tables with paper coverings groaned beneath the weight of food provided by the townspeople. Matt himself had made a contribution: a tub of fried chicken from a fast-food store.

Fishing out his preferred brand of beer, he ignored Dylan's running commentary about one thing or another and instead watched Laura talking to Marilyn Rogers, the mayor. Marilyn cocked her silver head attentively, apparently enthralled by whatever the lovely Mrs. Gilliam might be saying.

And she *was* lovely. Matt had thought so the moment he saw her, a new employee at his grandfather's newspaper. But he knew she was a widow, and out of respect for her loss he'd waited a year before he asked her out—a whole year. It hadn't been easy, either, because he'd been intrigued by her from the first.

On their one and only date, they'd gone to the popular local saloon called the Painted Pony, had dinner and even danced a little. He'd found her quiet, almost shy, which didn't jibe with any of the newspaper people *he'd* ever known. But then, he'd decided she was probably just intimidated because he was her boss's grandson.

He was also owner of his own successful construction company and proud of the town where he'd been born and raised. He worked hard for the Rawhide Chamber of Commerce and the local Kids' Club and every other civic issue that came along, and had donated the labor to erect the bandstand in the park. In short, he was very involved in community life.

She wasn't, outside of her work. And despite her beauty, he hadn't exactly seen guys knocking down her door to get friendly. Most of the eligible men in town were probably put off by her aloof manner, but not Matt.

Something told him that with a little effort, she could relax enough to be a whole lot of fun—and he was more than willing to help her. That's why, when he took her home, he pulled her into his arms and kissed her.

It was a nice kiss—a *real* nice kiss. For a moment, she'd felt compliant and warm in his arms. Her lips were incredibly soft beneath his, and unexpectedly he felt something…something *hopeful* flip over in his chest…something like his heart. The kiss was so much more than he'd expected!

Breathless and shocked, he'd pulled back to stare down at her face, illuminated by the porch light. She looked dazed, and for a moment her fingers clutched at his arms. But just as he was opening his mouth to tell her he thought she was just about the greatest thing since sliced bread, she yanked away, gave him a withering look and slapped him so hard his jaw still ached just thinking about it.

Needless to say, there had been no more dates with Laura Gilliam, nor would there be. The slap said it all; you didn't have to hit Matt Reynolds over the head with a two-by-four.

But over the intervening months, he'd found himself reliving that incident and wondering what had happened. Because something still whispered to him that if she ever let herself go—

Dylan stepped in front of Matt and yelled in his face. "Hey! You heard a word I've been sayin'?"

"No." Matt snapped out of his trip down memory lane. "Was it important?"

Dylan grimaced. "I just asked you a question, is all."

"Care to run it by me one more time?"

"I just wanna know if Brandee is your date today or are you free to get into trouble with the rest of us boys?" Dylan winked broadly.

Matt sensed a friendly poker game in the offing and felt a moment's regret. "Yeah, Brandee's coming later."

Dylan did not look happy to hear it. "Isn't that gettin' just a little too serious?"

Matt recoiled. "No! I got more sense than that. Dammit, Dylan, I just got tired of her chasin' me. She's been after me for years, although God knows why. I just finally got tired of runnin'."

"It's probably the old 'football hero and the cheerleader' thing," Dylan agreed. "Just watch your step, buddy. She can be real unpredictable."

Dylan led the way toward a group of men clustered around a horse someone had ridden in on, and Matt fell in beside him. But his thoughts were elsewhere, on the woman who seemed intent on tracking him down, and the *other* woman who didn't even like to be in the same room with him.

Damn but life was strange, and women were stranger still.

"Hi, Miz Gilliam, can Zach come play with us kids?"

Laura looked around to find Jessica Reynolds grinning at her. "Well," she said, "I'm not sure—"

"*Please,* Mama?" Zach inserted.

Aware that she was frequently called overprotective, Laura tried to calm fears she knew were completely unfounded. Bravely she asked, "Will you keep an eye on him, Jessica?"

"Sure!" The girl pushed all that long hair behind her ears. "We won't go far."

"All right. Would you like me to put your hair up into a ponytail before you go?"

"Would you?" Jessica's eyes sparkled. "I've got a rubber band but I kind of get it tangled up when I try to do it."

"Oh, dear." Laura took the rubber band from the girl, a plain one that looked as if it had come off a copy of the Rawhide *Review.* "This really isn't the best kind to use," she explained, carefully slipping it around the handful of hair at the back of Jessica's head. "I'll pick up the kind you need next chance I get."

"Thanks!" Jessica turned, rose on tiptoe, and planted a quick kiss on her benefactress's cheek. "Come on, Zach!"

Laura watched the two kids rush away to join the mob chasing after a soccer ball in the middle of the grassy area. What a sweet child. Matt was a lucky—

She pulled herself up short. Thinking about Matt just annoyed her, and had since the one and only time she'd gone out with him. *Was she holding out on him?* Much more than an apple pie!

The nerve of the man, to think she'd fall into his arms for the price of a simple dinner at the local gathering place a couple of years ago. Of course, it *had* been nice dancing with him. He moved with an athlete's grace and his arms had felt strong around her. The brush of his thighs against hers as they moved in perfect unison sent little tingles running through her from the very first step. Matt Reynolds, she'd admitted to herself, was a very sexy man.

Which didn't give him any right to think he could grab her like some caveman while they stood before her front door. All right, the pressure of those firm lips on hers had made her…almost giddy for a moment. And maybe she'd clung to him a bit longer than she should have—in shock, nothing more.

Apparently he wasn't accustomed to dating *ladies,* because he'd looked absolutely stupefied when she slapped his face.

After that—

"Hi. What's got *you* looking so serious?"

Laura pulled herself together to smile at her best friend, Katy Andrews, city reporter for the *Review.* Black-haired and green-eyed Katy had the suspicious nature you'd expect of a news reporter. Laura herself lacked that attribute, so had settled happily into lifestyles.

"I was just thinking about work," Laura lied. "I've got to go back in to write the Citizen of the Year story for Sunday's newspaper, and I'll have to make arrangements for someone to keep an eye on Zach."

"I'll watch him for you."

"Really? I'd appreciate that. It won't take me long."

"Take as long as you like. He's a great kid and we always have a good time."

"Then thank you, I accept. Do you have any idea when they'll get this show on the road?"

"You mean, announce the Citizen of the Year? After we eat." Katy glanced around. "There's Matt and Dylan!" She waved and smiled.

"Talk about looking for trouble," Laura remarked dryly.

Katy laughed. "With Dylan, yes, but Matt's okay." She winked. "You could do worse, you know."

"I'd rather go over Niagara Falls in a barrel," Laura cried.

"Okay, let Brandee have him, then. Why not? She's been after him since second grade."

"With pleasure." But Laura felt a shiver run through her at the thought of Matt at the mercy of Brandee Haycox, who seemed like a woman accustomed to getting what—or who—she went after.

"Speaking of love and romance…"

"Is that what we were speaking of?"

"More or less. But speaking of it, what did you think about that classified in yesterday's paper?"

"What classified?"

Katy's green eyes widened. "Don't tell me you missed it! Everyone in town's talking about it."

"Don't keep me in suspense."

"It's from some guy who signs himself Prince Charming. He's looking for a wife who's pretty and nice and likes kids." She grinned. "Is that cute or what?"

"I'd call it strange. A newspaper ad is hardly an acceptable way to find a wife."

"Don't be a spoilsport." Katy wrinkled her nose. "I'm thinking about applying, actually."

"Katy!" Laura stared at her friend, appalled. "You wouldn't!"

"Why not? Hey, twenty-nine-year-olds have to grab the brass rings where they can find them. Besides, it's probably someone I already know, just too shy to come right out and say he wants to get married and have kids."

"Maybe it's Dylan," Laura suggested with a laugh.

"Maybe it's not," Katy shot back. "It could be Matt, I suppose, but he's got more women than he can shake a stick at *without* putting an ad in the newspaper. I've come up with a few other possibilities, though...."

Laura listened politely to Katy's list of prospective Prince Charmings but her attention kept wandering to the group of men clustered around the red horse, and to one tall, broad-shouldered man in particular....

"Attention, everybody! Your attention please!" Mayor Marilyn Rogers stood on the bandstand, hands held up to quiet the crowd milling around below. When the level of sound had dropped to a murmur, she went on. "As you know, the purpose of this community picnic is to announce the selection of our Citizen of the Year, a great honor that goes to the man or woman who best exemplifies the unselfish ideals of service...."

Laura, standing unobtrusively near one corner of

the bandstand, zoned out. This was the third such event she'd covered and she pretty much knew the mayor's spiel by heart. Not that she didn't take it seriously; she did. She considered community service to be the sacred duty of every good citizen, and always tried to do her part.

But at the moment, she just wished Marilyn would announce the winner because Laura had to interview him or her, then rush back to the office and—

"—this year's coveted award goes to the man who spearheaded efforts to revitalize the downtown area...the man who chaired revision to the city's general plan...the man who headed up the fund drive to refurbish the gymnasium at the Rawhide Boys and Girls Club. Ladies and gentlemen, Rawhide's Citizen of the Year...*Matt Reynolds!*"

Laura's heart stood still. Not Matt! She didn't want to interview him. But automatically she turned toward the spot where he'd been standing. He looked as stunned as she. Dylan slapped him on the back and gave him a shove. Reluctantly Matt moved forward to accept his plaque to the sound of enthusiastic applause.

Now he'll probably say some arrogant thing about how it's high time he won, Laura thought disapprovingly. Some people were just too sure of themselves.

Marilyn handed him the plaque, which was actually a leather-wrapped slab with all the particulars burned into it—get it? John had asked with delight the first time she'd seen it. *Rawhide!*

When Matt looked up to face the applause, his expression was serious, not arrogant at all. In fact, it looked as if he had to swallow hard before he could find his voice.

Even then, all he said was, "Thank you—thank you all. I don't deserve this but I appreciate you folks giving it to me." He sucked in a deep breath. "I know it's a cliché but…" His gaze wandered over the faces in the throng, settling in on Laura's for a heart-stopping instant that made her catch her breath.

After a moment he went on in a low, even humble, voice. "This town has given me so much that it's only fair for me to try to give back what little I can. It takes all of us to make Rawhide the kind of place where we're happy to live and bring up our kids. If I've helped at all, I'm deeply grateful for the opportunity. And for this."

He waved the plaque above his head, grinned and stepped off the bandstand.

Laura stood frozen to the spot for a moment. Then her background and training surged to the fore. She stepped in front of him when he would have returned to his spot.

"Excuse me," she said through the tumult of sound, "but I need a little information for the *Review*. If you have a moment…?"

For an instant, she thought he might turn her down. But then he grinned and said a cocky, "Sure. I try never to disappoint a lady."

She could have kicked him for that.

It was easy enough to get the who-what-where-when-why of it—the classic five W's of journalism. But getting to the man beneath was considerably harder, for a variety of reasons.

For one thing, the interview was conducted sitting side by side on the edge of the bandstand, with well-wishers feeling free to wander past to admire Matt's plaque and offer congratulations. For another, he'd reverted to his old sardonic self. Only when Jessica and Zach rushed up to give him hugs did he relax into soft good humor again.

Jessica beamed. "I'm proud of you, Daddy!" she announced.

Zach parroted her: "I'm proud of you, too, Da—" Stricken, he glanced at his mom and hurriedly changed it to, "Mr. Reynolds."

The near miss was like an arrow to Laura's heart but it didn't seem to faze Matt, who sent both children on their way with hugs and kisses. When they were gone, Laura couldn't help observing, "You're very good with children."

He shrugged. "I like 'em, that's all."

"At least we have one thing in common."

He looked at her through suddenly narrow blue eyes. "I think we have considerably more than *that* in common."

Her heart skipped a beat. "Not a chance. Tell me, have you lived your entire life in Rawhide?"

He nodded. "Except for a few years at the University of Colorado."

"Your family…?"

He looked thoughtful. "My dad died four years ago and my mom moved back to Oklahoma City, where her people are. You know my grandpa and my daughter.''

She couldn't miss the pride in his voice at mention of his daughter. Softly she asked, "And your wife?"

He grimaced as if with remembered pain. "She…had a medical problem and died when Jessica was only a baby." His gaze sharpened. "How about you? Your husband…?"

"An accident while jogging." She looked away. "The car didn't even slow down."

"That's really tough, Laura. Where were you living at the time?"

"Chicago." Her voice was barely a whisper.

"Is that why you moved to Rawhide?"

She nodded, belatedly realizing she'd lost control of the interview. "W-when did you start your construction company? Did you—?"

"I don't want to talk about that," he said. "I want to know more about you. What did your husband do?"

"He was an attorney and don't ask any more questions!" She glared at him, jabbing her pen point against the paper in her reporter's notebook. "I've got enough for my story." She closed her reporter's notebook with a snap. "Thanks for your time and congratulations again on—"

"Laura!" Katy hurried up. "Would you do me a favor?"

Laura nodded. "Of course."

Katy offered a couple of folded pages from her reporter's notebook. "Could you take this back to the office and leave it on John's desk? That's where everything sent to Box 100 ends up.''

"Katy!'' Laura stared at her. "You didn't!''

"Didn't what?'' Matt looked from one to the other.

Katy looked pleased with herself. "I answered Prince Charming's ad.''

"You what?'' Matt looked clueless.

"Oh, Matt!'' Katy shook her head as if in disappointment. "If you don't know about the ad, you're one of the few who doesn't. It's a Classified, from Prince Charming looking for a wife who is nice and pretty and who likes kids and animals.''

He looked aghast. "Some guy actually put in a Want Ad for a wife? I don't believe it.''

"It's true.'' Laura backed up her friend.

"But there are women all over the place,'' he argued. "Why would anyone have to advertise to find one?''

Katy glared at him. "Come on, Matt, say what you mean—that women are a dime a dozen.''

"You said that, not me.''

Laura had had enough. She stood up. "I'm going back to the office. Katy, give me your application, and I'll turn it in.''

Matt shook his head disapprovingly. "What kind of man would run an ad like that?''

"I'm assuming that's a rhetorical question,'' Laura said. She turned to Katy. "Shall I pick Zach up here or at your place?''

"Don't go,'' Matt said quickly. "Before Katy busted in, I was about to ask what it would take to get a piece of that apple pie Zach told me about.''

Before Laura could respond, a honey-coated voice that could only belong to Brandee Haycox, local femme fatale, interrupted. "This I've *got* to hear."

Matt wanted to groan but didn't. He'd been enjoying Laura's company before everybody and her sister busted in on them. Nevertheless, he stood up and gave Brandee a peck on the temple; after all, she was his date, at least technically.

"Hi, Brandee," he greeted her. "Glad you could make it." And only a little sarcasm crept into his tone, although she was four hours and eleven minutes late.

"Really?" Her thin brows curved up. Unlike most of the women here today, she wore a sundress instead of pants or jeans. Her feet were encased in spike-heeled sandals. She'd been dressing fancy since grammar school.

"Yes, really."

She rolled her eyes. "You seemed to be having a great time without me."

He *had* been having a great time, he realized. Finally he'd satisfied at least a little of his curiosity about Laura.

But chivalry made him say, "Nah. I was just doing my duty."

At which point, Laura waved her notebook in the air. "I just interviewed Matt for tomorrow's paper," she explained.

"Why?" Brandee wanted to know. "Did he rob a bank?"

Laura almost smiled at that one. "No, but you're getting warm. He just won Citizen of the Year."

"Really? You did?" She threw her arms around Matt's neck and gave him a big kiss on the cheek, then pulled back to scrub at the lipstick stain with one beautifully manicured fingertip. "I'm so glad because now I won't feel so guilty breaking up with you!"

CHAPTER THREE

LAURA was looking straight at Jessica when Brandee made her stunning announcement. The little girl had slipped up to hover behind her father instead of joining the circle—eavesdropping, it was clear to Laura.

But the satisfaction on Jessica's face now was eye-opening to say the least. The girl was overjoyed! Laura's heart went out to her. She'd obviously felt threatened by her father's girlfriend, rightly or wrongly. Did that mean she'd resent any woman who might enter Matt's life, temporarily or permanently?

Not that it mattered to Laura, of course, except that Jessica so obviously needed a woman's guidance. It would be awful if the right woman came along and the little girl rejected her.

Matt finally found his voice. "You're *what?*" he demanded of Brandee.

"Breaking up with you, darling." She touched his cheek lightly with one graceful hand. "I know I've chased you shamelessly for years but something's come up." Her smile sparkled. "I'm moving to Denver to manage a new health club Daddy just bought me." A tiny frown line appeared between her perfectly made-up eyes. "I don't think I could stand a long-distance relationship, do you? I was just waiting for the right time to tell you and this is it." She beamed at all and sundry.

Katy said, "Ye Gods!" very softly.

Laura said, "This is personal. I think I'll just run along and give you two privacy."

Brandee waved such discretion aside. "No need. We've said all that needs saying." She added belatedly, "Haven't we, Matt?"

Matt blinked as if he were still trying to come to terms with her brush-off. "Yeah, I guess we have." He took a deep breath, then grinned. "Good luck, Brandee. I hope everything goes the way you want it to."

Her smile was radiant. "Aren't you a sweetie! I'll miss you, you good-lookin' thing." Another light kiss, this time on his mouth; then she turned and sashayed away.

They stared after her, then they stared at Matt. He still looked stunned. The silence stretched out uncomfortably until it was finally broken by Jessica.

"Ya-hoo!" She flung herself at her father's back, catching him by surprise when she hugged him fiercely around the waist. "We don't need her, Daddy! Just you wait and see—!"

"Hey," Dylan said, "did you ever dodge a bullet! Brandee's chased you for so long that when she finally caught you, I was afraid your goose was really cooked."

Matt had just filled his friend in on Brandee's surprise announcement, and the two were loitering beneath a shady tree while the picnic wound down around them.

"Yeah, I was a little worried myself." Matt took

a deep pull on his beer. "It was kind of a shock, though," he admitted.

"Kinda hurts your feelings, gettin' dumped more or less in public."

Matt shrugged, but he wasn't thinking about the "public." He was thinking about Laura, who'd looked so disapproving. "Jessica was kinda obvious about her feelings on the subject," he said. "Brandee just wasn't the motherly type."

Dylan laughed. "You can say that again!"

"Yeah, well, it's over. This dating stuff can be a real pain, you know? I think I'll just take my time before I get mixed up with another woman."

"Sure," Dylan said, "you do that."

John invited Laura to join him for coffee in his office Monday morning. "Just wanted to tell you what a fine job you did on that Citizen of the Year story about my grandson in Sunday's paper," he said. "I know it's not easy, writing about the boss's kin, but you handled it just fine."

"Thanks," Laura said, truly grateful because it *had* been a difficult story. At least she could be proud she hadn't let her personal feelings about the man show through. Actually, she'd felt kind of sorry for him, being dumped in public that way.

"So," John said, "how do you think the picnic went? Seemed to me folks were having a good time— at least until we ran out of beer."

Laura laughed. "I don't think that hurt the event in the slightest. Actually, I think everyone had a great time."

"Pick up any good gossip?"

She thought for a moment. "Not really," she confessed. "Everyone was too busy discussing the Prince Charming ad to get into much of anything else."

John frowned into his coffee cup. "There *is* a lot of interest in that, all right."

From the open doorway, Matt's voice surprised them. "A lot of interest in *what?*"

Laura realized instantly that he thought they'd been talking about him. She hastened to set his mind at ease. "About the Prince Charming ad," she said. "It was a hot topic of conversation at the picnic Sunday."

His lip curled with disdain. He looked big and tough and impatient this morning in his faded jeans and red plaid work shirt. "I pity the poor guy who placed that ad when his identity comes out—and it will. It always does."

"Why?" Laura frowned. "I think the ad is kind of sweet."

"Sweet!" Matt rolled his eyes. "He's gonna deserve what he gets, if you ask me. And what he's gonna get is a women who can't get a man any other way—that is, if anyone besides Katy answers the ad at all."

Laura's temper soared. "What an arrogant thing to say!"

He shrugged. "I call 'em like I see 'em. Have there been any other responses, Granddad?"

"A few," John said evasively. "That's privileged information, by the way."

"Whatever." But Matt didn't look any less skeptical.

John cocked his head. "Did you drop by for a reason or are you just passing through?"

"I've got a reason all right—the usual." He turned to Laura. "There's going to be a delay in delivery of that fancy hardware you want for your family room. I told you it might take a little extra time to get that particular faucet but—"

"Oh, good grief!" She glared at him. "Just how long is 'a little extra time'?"

He shrugged. "A week, maybe ten days."

She gritted her teeth.

"So what do you want me to do?" he pressed.

"I want you to wait for it! I want what I want!"

"Yeah," he muttered, "you want what you want *when you want it*. This time it ain't gonna happen."

She changed her tactics. "Then we'll just have to cope, won't we?" But she said it very sweetly.

He practically growled at her, then turned abruptly and disappeared through the open door. He nearly bumped into Mayor Rogers, who was entering.

"Matt!" she called after him. "Matt, I want to talk to—"

But he was gone. She entered, shrugging. "I'll track him down later," she said cheerfully. "In the meantime, I'm delighted to find the two of you together."

John waved her toward a seat. "How so, Madame Mayor?"

"Because now I'll only have to say this once." She took a seat and reached for the carafe of coffee on John's desk, poured some into a foam cup. "I'd like you both to come to my house Friday night for a kind of dinner party.''

John groaned. ''You know how I hate that sort of thing.''

Her sunny smile didn't waver. ''You'll like this one. It's a barbecue in the backyard.''

John hurrumphed. ''What's the occasion?''

''No occasion. I just enjoy breaking bread with a few of my favorite people now and again.'' She turned to Laura. ''Can you make it?''

''Of course.'' She wouldn't miss a social occasion at the mayor's house. Not only did she like Marilyn, but keeping abreast of the social scene in Rawhide was part of her job.

''Good.'' Marilyn grinned. ''Because I've also invited the new city planning director, who just happens to be available.''

Laura's first impulse was to groan, but then she asked herself, why not? Why not let the mayor play matchmaker? Laura wasn't doing too good a job of it on her own. After three years of widowhood, she was feeling somehow...lonesome.

Not that she wanted anything more than casual friendship. To love wholly and freely was to take an enormous risk. She'd lost one love; she wouldn't risk losing another.

She smiled. ''I love meeting new people,'' she said. ''Now if you'll both excuse me, I should get back to work before the boss realizes I'm goofing off.''

John waved her away. ''You do that.'' Before she was even out the door he was talking to Marilyn. ''Did you happen to see that little scene at the picnic between my grandson and the banker's ditzy daughter?''

"As a matter of fact, I did."

Laura stepped through the door, half closed it and paused. A quick glance around showed her that no one was in sight. If she just happened to bend down to retie her shoelace...

John: "There was no call for her to dump him in public."

Marilyn: "I think Matt can stand up to the strain. He's better off without her, John, and you know it."

John, sighing: "You got that right. But I worry about little Jessica. She needs a mother in the worst way."

Marilyn: "Not *that* kind of mother. It's very perceptive of you to figure that out, though."

John: "I didn't figure out nuthin', it hit me in the face. Dammit, Marilyn, someone ought to fix Matt up with a nice girl who'll be a mother to that child—"

Laura thought that no nice girl in her right mind would waste her time with a ladies' man like Matt Reynolds, even if Jessica *was* a nice little girl. Why, he'd probably been through every woman in town already, and he still—

April Forbes rounded the corner heading for her receptionist's desk. She stopped short at the sight of Laura kneeling beside the boss's half-closed door. "Everything all right?" she asked.

"Fine, just fine." Laura shot to her feet, her cheeks burning. "I just had to—" She pointed to her foot. "—shoelace, you know—gotta get back to work."

And she rushed out, leaving April staring after her.

*   *   *

The new planning director's name turned out to be Roger Reedy and *he* turned out to be a pleasant, if bland-looking, man in his mid-thirties. "I know you two will get on like gangbusters," the mayor said when she introduced them. "Just go on out back to the deck—you'll know everyone, Laura—and introduce Roger to anyone he hasn't met."

The doorbell rang at that moment so Laura nodded and led Roger away. She'd been in the mayor's home a couple of times before, so she knew her way around.

Sure enough, she recognized all those who'd arrived before her: John, of course, plus the president of the chamber of commerce and his wife, the superintendent of schools and his wife, the fire chief and his wife.

John was manning the barbecue when she led Roger up to him and began the introductions.

"We've met," John said, shaking hands. "So how's it going at city hall, Rog, old boy?"

Roger launched into an earnest explanation but Laura wasn't listening. Instead, her attention was drawn like a magnet to the man just pushing open the sliding-screen door.

Matt. Why should this surprise her? He was, after all, the newly crowned Citizen of the Year.

Their glances crossed paths, circled back and held. He looked great in crisp khaki trousers and a baby-blue Henley shirt, which was not to say he didn't look equally great in his usual uniform of jeans and work shirt. But he'd gotten a haircut and he looked sleek and commanding as he stood there in the open doorway.

He started toward her, or maybe he was heading for his grandfather. She'd never know because Marilyn appeared behind him and called his name. He stopped instantly, turning toward her.

Marilyn had a stranger with her: a tall, impressive thirty-something woman dressed all in black, her black hair pulled back in a tight bun. There was a strength about her face that was hardly traditional but she was intensely striking, Laura thought.

Marilyn's voice carried clearly. "Matt, I'd like you to meet Meredith Zink. She's new in town and I'm trying to help her meet a few people."

Matt took the hand the woman offered. "And what brings you to our fair city, Meredith?" he inquired.

"I'm an attorney," she said crisply. "I've just joined the law firm of Lowe and Winkler. Perhaps you know of them...?"

The two wandered off out of earshot. Marilyn stood there beaming as if she'd just pulled off a fabulous coup.

"—don't you agree, Laura?"

She snapped back to attention. "I beg your pardon, Roger?"

"I was just saying that I think Rawhide would be a wonderful place to raise children." He frowned. "You have a child, don't you? I thought someone said—"

"Yes, yes, I have a six-year-old son." A sudden thought struck her. "Do you like children, then?"

He nodded. "Very much. Of course, I don't have any, which is probably a good thing since I'm divorced. All I have is a dog, a Great Dane named Hamlet.''

She laughed politely at his wit but she was thinking, *likes kids and dogs.* Could she be talking to Prince Charming himself?

Matt heard Laura's light laughter and couldn't stop himself from sending a sharp glance in her direction, even though Meredith was elaborating on the various ins and outs of probate law. Laura looked wonderful in a flowery blue sundress that bared smooth golden shoulders. Her hair, a warm honey-blond, curled around her shoulders and framed her face perfectly.

Damn, it was a shame she was so self-righteous.

''—and then of course, when the family chooses to behave irrationally what's an attorney to do?'' Meredith spread her hands in a gesture that from another woman might be helpless. Coming from her, it looked more like a challenge.

''Absolutely,'' he agreed, thinking that he owed the mayor for this one. As a matchmaker, Marilyn was the pits.

Or at least, the pits where Matt was concerned. Laura, on the other hand, was gazing up at that planning geek as if he were the most brilliant man in the world.

Marilyn waved to get everyone's attention. ''Time to eat, folks,'' she sang out. ''Just pick up your utensils there—'' she pointed to a wooden picnic table ''—load up on salads and bread, then pass by John, the master barbecuer, who will dish up the ribs.''

Obediently they fell into line. Matt found himself

behind Meredith who was behind Laura who was behind the planning geek. Meredith promptly stuck out
her hand.

"I don't believe we've met. I'm Meredith Zink."

"Laura Gilliam. And this is Roger Reedy, the new
city planning director."

Roger turned with a smile on his face and froze.
Goodness, Matt thought in awe, it was just like one
of those shampoo commercials where the couple runs
through a field of daisies to throw themselves in each
other's arms. It was lightning striking.

It was love at first sight.

Their hands, their gazes, touched and clung. Laura
stood there looking baffled. Then the truth of the situation dawned on her and she stepped hastily aside.

Meredith took Laura's place behind Roger as
smoothly as if it had been preordained that she
should. "Roger," she said in a husky voice Matt had
not hitherto heard from her. "I'm simply *fascinated*
by the planning process."

Roger stared at her, lips parted. "And what do *you*
do, Meredith—besides take my breath away?"

Her laughter was as husky as her voice. "I'm an
attorney." It sounded like a downright sexy profes-
sion, the way it came out.

"My God!" He clasped her hand between both of
his. "I stand in awe of attorneys. Without them, our
world would be chaos...."

Matt looked at Laura and Laura looked at Matt and
as one, they burst out laughing. The other pair didn't
even notice as they drifted closer to the table of
goodies.

"Well," Matt said, "looks like it's just you and me, kid."

She groaned. "Why do these things always happen to me?"

"You mean, guys throwing you over for some other chick?"

"No, I mean nothing turning out the way it's supposed to. Mayor Rogers was trying to set him up with *me*."

"You'd go for that?"

She shrugged. "Why not? He's a perfectly respectable man—don't look so superior! She was obviously trying to set *you* up with Meredith."

A quick grin quirked the corners of his mouth. "I've been dumped on so much lately that I'm not even surprised it turned out this way."

They moved a step closer to the food and Laura said sincerely, "I'm sorry about what happened in the park with Brandee."

His brows rose. "Why? Easy come, easy go."

It sounded so flippant, as if one woman was much the same as another to him. "Well if that's how you feel about it—" she began stiffly.

He touched her arm lightly and she felt the shock all the way up her arm and into her shoulder.

"Don't be like that," he said, his voice and expression coaxing. "You take everything so serious and I was just kidding around. Look, our blind dates have run away together. Do you suppose we could get through this one evening without a major blowup?"

"You mean like...get along?"

He nodded.

"Be nice to each other?"

His nod this time was even more enthusiastic.

"Pretend we like each other?" She smothered a smile.

"Yeah," he said softly. "I know it's a stretch but...pretend."

A little shiver ran up her spine at the way he said that last word. Suddenly it occurred to her that she might not have to pretend quite as much as she'd supposed.

Fortunately they reached the table at that moment and she was able to avoid answering in the flurry of activity: collecting a plate, silverware, red-and-white-checked napkin. Then she had to deal with the food: potato salad, sliced tomatoes, baked beans, big fluffy yeast rolls with golden pats of butter.

At the large brick barbecue, John waited with his cook's fork held high. "So how's it going?" he asked Laura as he piled her plate with tender spare ribs.

"It's going fine but you're giving me too much food! I'll never eat all that," she complained, pulling her plate away.

Matt stepped up beside her. "Pile it on," he instructed his grandfather. "What she doesn't eat, I will."

"*You* will?" John's eyes went wide. "You mean you two are—" He looked at them askance.

"Certainly not!" Laura pulled herself up as tall as she could. "It's just that we've both been abandoned by our dinner partners and since we're all that's left—"

"That's a great way to put it," Matt broke in, holding his plate out for ribs. "I can be quite charming when I put my mind to it."

"I'll believe it when I see it," Laura muttered, turning away. But even as she said it, she knew she was lying.

Matt Reynolds was hard enough to resist when he was acting like a jerk. When he was being charming...

Matt *did* knock himself out to be charming, for all the good it did him. She was polite and pleasant but he could almost see her physically and emotionally pulling away from him. Okay, if that's how she wanted to be. He'd been caught in the same trap she had; they were both victims of a senior citizen matchmaker, that was all. Tomorrow they could go back to fighting over her damned family room.

In the meantime, Roger and Meredith were getting along like kindred souls. Matt cast a surreptitious glance their way. They'd chosen a spot in the shadows of a tall cottonwood tree. They weren't so much eating as gazing into each other's eyes with silly smiles on their faces.

He felt a pang of envy and turned quickly away. He couldn't imagine falling that hard and that fast for *anyone*. Which was just as well because his dinner companion didn't exactly inspire him in that direction.

Although she inspired him in *other* directions. Laura was a sexy little dish in this informal setting. If she ever gave him even a hint of encouragement...

He needed to change the subject, if only in his own mind. He leaned toward her and whispered in her ear. "You plan to eat any more of those ribs?"

"Be my guest." She shoved the plate toward him. "Although I don't know why you can't just go back for thirds."

He winced. "Thanks for announcing that, darlin'." He plucked the ribs from her plate with his fingers.

Across the picnic table from them, Marilyn smiled and nudged John with her elbow. "Isn't that cute? Laura's sharing her ribs with Matt."

John said, "Watch out for poison, Grandson!"

Everybody laughed, even Laura. "We're trying to get along just this one evening," she explained with a grimace. "But it's hard. Your grandson is no Prince Charming."

Matt groaned. "Thank God. Granddad, how many takers did you get on that cockamamie ad in the *Review?*"

The president of the chamber of commerce perked up. "Yeah, John, tell us about that. Everybody in town's talking about it. Who placed the ad, anyway?"

John shook his head. "You know I can't tell you that. We respect and protect the privacy of our advertisers, when they ask us to."

The other man laughed. "If I guess, will you tell me?"

"Nope."

"Just nod your head, blink your eyes, anything?"

"Nope."

"Was it Max Shipman?"

John didn't move a muscle.

"Was it Johnny Hurd?" the fire chief inquired.

"How about Tim Hatz? I saw him coming out of the newspaper office the other day with a big smirk on his face."

John looked disgusted. "He'd just sold a horse with a *Review* ad. The man got about twice what the nag was worth. You'd smirk, too."

"Well," Laura said, "whoever did it, I think the ad is very romantic."

"Romantic enough to answer?" Marilyn teased.

Laura recoiled. "Not hardly! I'm not looking for a husband, Prince Charming or otherwise."

Marilyn's eyes twinkled. "How about you, Matt? You've been awfully quiet. What do you think about Prince Charming?"

Matt grimaced. "Don't ask. I'm trying not to annoy this lady." He glanced at Laura, sitting beside him on the picnic bench.

"No, come on," the wife of the superintendent of schools chimed in. "I'd like a man's perspective on this. What *do* you think of a man who tries to find a wife in the Want Ads?"

Matt sucked in a deep breath, glanced at Laura, rolled his eyes and said, "He's gotta be nuts. Even when you're out there looking, it's hard enough to find someone you can put up with twenty-four hours a day."

"*Are* you looking, Matt?" someone called.

"Hell, no!" he flashed. "As I said, it's damned near impossible to find the right person in real life but in a newspaper ad? Gimme a break! The guy's a candidate for the loony bin."

Everybody laughed except Laura. Marilyn turned to John, who'd been quietly observing.

"So *has* anybody answered the ad? You can at least tell us that much."

"Okay, but that's all you'll get out of me. There have been seven responses."

A shocked silence fell over the little group and then the chamber president let out a long low whistle. "I don't know what this says about Rawhide women," he announced, "but it sure says something."

"I think," his wife shot back, and she didn't sound as if she was joking, "I think it says Rawhide women are hungry for a little romance—starting with this one."

"Ah, honey—"

Matt looked down at his plate but not before Laura saw the smile playing around his mouth. At that moment, Meredith and Roger interrupted to say their goodbyes to Marilyn. They were still so wrapped up in each other that they couldn't get away fast enough.

If Roger was Prince Charming, Laura thought, he sure wasn't waiting for the results of his ad!

"Sorry about that," the mayor said when they'd gone. "I thought I was doing something good for the both of you but you know what they say about the best laid plans."

"Not to worry," Matt soothed her. "I need a challenge once in a while to stay sharp." He darted an amused glance at Laura.

"I like a challenge, too," she said sweetly, "and I have hopes that someday I'll find one."

Matt joined in the general laughter, even though it was at his expense.

"Not to change the subject," Marilyn said to John, "but I've promised the use of the cabin to friends from Denver next week. Any problem with that?"

John thought a minute. "Sounds okay."

Laura frowned but said nothing. Marilyn noticed her curiosity nonetheless.

"John and my husband bought a log cabin together in the mountains years ago," she said. "Our two families would take turns using it until all our kids grew up and moved away. Since Tom—that's my late husband—died, it pretty much sits unused. So we're always happy to find people who'd like a nice, relaxing week or two away from all the pressures of civilization, right, John?"

He nodded. "The more the merrier, I always say. Any of you ever want to use it, just speak up."

The chamber president nodded. "My wife and I were up there last summer on a second honeymoon and it was great," he said enthusiastically.

His wife, who was still glowering at him about the "romance" issue, added, "But we won't be needing it this year, will we, *dear!*"

Laura smiled at the exchange but her mind was racing. Her vacation was coming up soon and she'd planned to stay home to can tomatoes and maybe freeze a few peaches. But with construction proceeding so slowly on her family room, the quiet delights of a cabin in the Rocky Mountains was mesmerizing.

Peace and quiet—just what she and Zach needed...

CHAPTER FOUR

MATT showed up Monday morning before Zach and Laura had even finished breakfast. At the sight of him, her heart sunk. He had one of those grim ready-to-face-the-worst expressions.

She eyed him warily. "Will a cup of coffee help?"

He shrugged. "I doubt it, but it can't hurt. Are you offering?"

"Sure." She stepped away from the kitchen door and gestured him inside.

Zach grinned over his spoonful of cold cereal. "Hi, Mr. Reynolds. Can I be your helper today?"

Matt ruffled the boy's hair. "Afraid not today, partner. That's what I came to talk to your mother about."

Laura finished pouring his coffee and carried it to the table. "Something tells me this is *not* good news."

"I'm afraid not." He shoveled two spoonfuls of sugar into his cup.

She noticed he was going to great lengths to keep from looking at her. She sat back down and gestured him to do the same, which he did. He'd never been in her small sunny kitchen before and he seemed to fill it with his presence. He was such a physically commanding man, she thought uncomfortably. There was just something about him....

He cleared his throat and faced her at last. "I'm afraid I'm going to have to stop work here for a couple of days—maybe as long as a week."

"What!" She bolted straight upright in her chair. "Why?"

"Because we have an emergency on another building site and I'm the only one who can handle it."

"But—but—!" She sputtered to a halt until she could contain herself. "That's pretty poor planning, if you ask me. Maybe a little time management is in order here."

For a moment he met her outraged gaze, his own almost pensive. He glanced at Zach, who was watching and listening avidly, before going on. "Laura," he said carefully, "have you noticed that I'm pretty much building your room addition single-handedly?"

She frowned. "Now that you mention it…"

"There's a *reason*. You tend to drive my workers…" Another glance at Zach. "C-r-a-z-y." He spelled it out.

Zach scrunched up his face. "C-r-z—"

"Never mind, dear." Laura hastily patted his arm. To Matt she said coolly, "You're kidding, of course."

"Afraid not." He took a sip from his cup. "Good coffee."

"Don't try to change the subject." She turned to her son. "Zach, why don't you go pick up those toys you left in the living room last night while I talk to Mr. Reynolds."

"Do I *have* to?"

"You have to," she said firmly.

He went, but not happily and with many a resentful backward glance. When she judged him out of ear-shot, Laura swung on Matt.

"What do you mean, I drive your men crazy!"

"Just that. A man doesn't like a woman hanging over his shoulder saying— Forgive me, Laura, but saying stupid things."

"Such as?" Her jaws were so tight she could barely speak.

"Such as, 'Why are you putting that nail there? Don't you think it should go over here? And that insulation doesn't look nearly thick enough. Don't you think we should double it? Have my light fixtures come in yet? They're solid gold set with diamonds, you know.'"

By the time he'd finished, her cheeks burned with resentment. "I never once said my light fixtures were gold set with diamonds!"

His laughter sounded relieved. "I just threw that in to see if you were listening. I notice you don't deny the rest of it."

"Well...not entirely." She pressed her lips together in an annoyed line. "I don't know why your workers are so touchy," she burst out. "They should be open to good suggestions."

"Laura, your suggestions are *not* good. They're annoying. These men are professionals." He cocked his head. "How many houses have you built, anyway?"

"Sarcasm does not become you," she sniffed. "All right, I get the point. I don't like it or agree with it but I get it. So that's why you're doing the work yourself?"

"No, that's why nobody else is willing to work here, even if I pay them a bonus."

She gasped. "That's insulting!"

"That's what they said." He finished his coffee and placed the cup on the table. "Anyway, I'll get your job done and it'll be a good one, but I've got to do it myself. Unless—" He brightened. "Any chance you're going away for a week or so of vacation anytime soon? I could get in here with a full crew and wrap this up."

"As a matter of fact—" She chewed on her lip, mulling over her options. "I'll have to let you know for sure, but yes, there's a very good possibility."

"Great." He rose. "In the meantime, I'll do as much as I can, when I can."

"Darn it, Matt!" She also stood. "This may be small potatoes to you but it's very important to me. I'm sure it's the only room I'll ever add to this house so it's got to be perfect."

He shook his head almost wearily. "None of my jobs are small potatoes to me," he said. "You'll get the best I'm capable of giving you—and I'm good, damned good." His square chin thrust out at an angle which dared her to argue that point. When she didn't, he went on. "But perfect—" He shook his head. "I'm not real sure perfect exists."

"It certainly does, and I want it!"

She wanted perfect in her new family room, at work, and most of all, in her life. The fact that she had yet to find perfection any place at all did nothing to dissuade her from seeking it.

*   *   *

Matt deliberately waited until the noon hour to drop
by his grandfather's office. The last thing he wanted
was another set-to with the difficult Mrs. Gilliam.
Once a day was about as much as he could handle.

"The boss is out but he should be back soon,"
Mrs. Forbes said. "You can go on in and wait, if you
like."

Matt debated. Just then, he saw Laura walk into the
hall from the editorial department. His reluctance to
confront her again so soon made up his mind in a
hurry.

"I'll do that," he told the receptionist. "And
thanks."

She smiled and answered a ringing phone. Matt
walked into the office and half closed the door.

His grandfather had started the Rawhide *Review* as
a young man, and no one else had ever been at the
helm. John Reynolds knew every person and every
secret in town, it seemed, and he dispensed journal-
istic justice wherever he saw fit.

Matt had grown up in awe of his grandpa. Perhaps
his father had felt the same way because once Matt
and his sister, Sarah, were grown, he and Matt's
mother had moved away for good. Sarah had married
and done the same, but Matt had stayed.

He couldn't imagine being happy anywhere else.

Lately, he couldn't imagine being happy, period.

Wandering to a window, he looked out on
Rawhide's main street. Across the way he saw the
police chief standing on the sidewalk before the police station, talking earnestly to the owner of the
Rawhide Insurance Agency. Further down the block,

the mayor and the new planning director—the one who'd filched Matt's date at the barbecue—were walking this way, deep in conversation.

This was a good place to live, a good place to raise children.

It was not necessarily a good place to find a soul mate. Not that he'd been working at that very hard, but sometimes he had to wonder if a woman, the right woman, might fill that tiny hole left in his heart by the death of Jessica's mother....

Turning, his idle glance fell upon his grandfather's messy desk. A small papier-mâché airplane caught his eye and he smiled. He'd made that himself, in the third grade, if he remembered correctly. And the framed red paper heart was Jessica's work, done last Valentine's Day for the great-grandfather she adored, and who adored her.

What he *didn't* understand was what her red-and-white ceramic pig was doing on Grandpa's desk. Ah, well, the two were always working on some scheme or another together.

How did John find anything in this mess, Matt wondered. Not that he himself was particularly neat but this was ridiculous. If he didn't know better, he'd think—

His eyes widened. The file on the top of the stack was labeled "Prince Charming." Answers to that crazy ad, he thought; had to be.

It would be wrong for him to pick up the file, wrong of him to open it, wrong of him to pull out the top sheet of paper—

"To hell with it," he muttered, doing just that. He wouldn't tell anyone. No one would ever know that—

"Matthew Reynolds, what are you doing, going through your grandfather's private files?"

He started and looked up guiltily to find the outraged Laura Gilliam glaring at him from the doorway. But he didn't replace the file. "It's all right," he said. "I know the boss."

"That doesn't give you any special privileges around here." She walked into the room. "That's the Prince Charming file, isn't it?"

What was she, psychic? "Yeah," he muttered. "How did you know?"

"Because I was in here talking to John not ten minutes ago and he had it out. He said it was just about time to turn the file over to Prince Charming for a decision."

"In that case, there's no reason I shouldn't have a look first." Matt snatched out the top sheet of paper.

"Don't!" Laura lunged for the page.

He lifted it above her head. "What are you so worked up about?" An incredible thought occurred to him. "Did you answer the ad? Is that what's got you so—"

She turned away sharply. "Certainly not. It's just that…" She whirled back to face him. "I don't think it's very nice to have fun at the expense of a man who's obviously very sincere."

"That's not what I'm doing. I'm just curious. Hell, everybody in town is curious." He looked at the sheet of paper and read aloud, "'Dear Prince Charming. Do I know you? I know everyone in town, just about.

Are you walking around looking like all the other jerky guys around here?'''

Matt glanced up at Laura, frowning. "That's not a very nice thing to say about us Rawhide men."

"But richly justified," she said too sweetly. "Please, put that letter back where you got it."

He read right over her protests.

"'Are you hiding your romantic tendencies? A girl can always dream.... But to get on to specifics, I like kids and dogs. I don't know if I'd call myself pretty but—'"

John's voice floated through the open door. "I'll be in my office the rest of the day in case anyone needs me, April."

Matt fumbled for the file. "We'll deny everything!"

"I have nothing to deny!" Laura also reached for the file. "Here, let me do that, you'll never—"

Their hands collided and the file fumbled free. It fell on the floor, numerous sheets of paper sliding out across the blue carpet. Matt and Laura dropped to their knees and grabbed for the manila folder simultaneously. Their hands met, tangled, locked together. Her shocked gaze met his and time stood still. For one crazy moment, the urge to haul her into his arms was nearly irresistible.

John entered the room and stopped short.

"He caught us!" Matt whispered. Releasing her hand reluctantly, he scooped up the spilled contents of the folder.

John stood over them. "Have I interrupted anything important?" he inquired, his tone dry.

Laura scrambled to her feet, her movements jerky. "Certainly not. We were just—I—that is, he was—" She stopped, apparently defeated by the intricacies of the situation.

Matt finished stacking the sheets and stood up, the folder in his hand. "We noticed Prince Charming's file and thought we might as well check it out."

"That's a barefaced lie," Laura exclaimed. "I didn't have anything to do with it, John. In fact, I tried to stop him."

"Did you now." John looked skeptical.

"I did, honestly." She glared at Matt. "Tell your grandfather the truth," she ordered. "I refuse to take the blame for something I didn't do."

He didn't have the heart to tease her anymore. "She's right, Granddad," he admitted. "I was copping a peek and she caught me. She tried to get me to stop, but since it was all in good clean fun, I naturally ignored her. I mean, what could it hurt?"

John looked annoyed. "Prince Charming has a right to his privacy, don't you think?"

"Why?" Matt really didn't understand. "Newspapers are public, right? When you put something into the newspaper, you can't really expect it to remain a secret, can you?"

"That's the way you figure it, is it?" John plucked the file from Matt's hand.

Matt shrugged. "That's the only reasonable way *to* see it."

John took his seat behind the desk. "You were pretty outspoken in your scorn for Prince Charming at the mayor's barbecue, if I remember correctly."

"I wouldn't exactly call it scorn," Matt hedged. He was all too aware of Laura's disapproving presence at his side. She sure looked good today, her eyes all bright and sparkly from their sparring match. "I'd call it more..."

"Disdain?" Laura suggested. "Contempt?"

They both looked at him as if he'd kicked a puppy. A little more of this and they might start to hurt his feelings. "I'd call it more pity," he defended himself. "What kind of guy has to put an ad in the newspaper to find a woman?"

"Not just a woman," Laura reminded softly, "a *wife*. At least his intentions are honorable."

"Like mine aren't?" He was getting plenty annoyed here.

Laura shrugged. "If the shoe fits—"

"Stop fighting, children." John placed the file on the desk. He waited until they'd settled down before he went on. "Regardless of what you may think of the wisdom of placing a lonely hearts ad, I assume you all would agree that the die has been cast and Prince Charming should honor his implied contract to carefully consider the responses of women who'd like to meet him."

"Yeah, sure." Matt could care less what Prince Charming did.

"Laura?"

"Absolutely." She gave her head a sharp nod for emphasis. "Think how humiliated all those women would be if he didn't." Her eyes went wide. "And think how unhappy people in this town would be if they never found out who this Prince Charming really is.''

''Oh, yeah,'' Matt said, ''we definitely should 'out' this guy—I mean, he should come clean.'' He frowned at his grandfather. ''So where are you going with this?''

''Not much farther.'' John offered the file to his grandson.

Who made no move to take it, instead asking suspiciously, ''What's going on here? What are you up to now?''

''Take it,'' John ordered.

''Why should I?'' There was something fishy about this. Reluctantly Matt reached for the file.

''Because,'' John said, ''your daughter placed that ad. Congratulations, Matthew. You're Prince Charming.''

Matt looked as if he were about to keel over. All the color left his face and he gaped at his grandfather with a face suffused with horror.

Laura almost felt sorry for him. Almost.

He started to speak but his voice was a croak. He cleared his throat and tried again. ''Jessica placed that ad? My own *daughter* is making a laughingstock of me? I can't believe it.''

''Believe it.'' John's face softened. ''Jessica's a smart little girl. She needs a mother and she knows it.''

''But—?'' Matt's puzzlement was clear.

''She came in here with her piggy bank and asked

me to run an ad she'd written all by herself. I couldn't turn her down.''

Matt's blue eyes flashed. "You could have called me and told me. I *am* her father."

"And I'm her grandfather, so we both want what's best for her—and for you."

Laura stirred in her chair. "I think it's adorable," she said, "a little girl trying to take care of her daddy."

John nodded. "Jessica and I agreed we'd keep this our little secret until we found out whether or not there'd be any takers. Since there were—"

Matt looked down at the folder as if it were a snake coiled to strike. "So what am I supposed to do with this?" he demanded.

"Look over the responses and pick one," John suggested dryly.

"No way! I'm not looking for a wife."

"You should be," John shot back, "because you need one almost as much as Jess needs a mother."

Matt's expression turned bleak. "Have I been such a bad father, then?"

"Great father, not so hot as a mother." John's gaze was tender. "Jessica is getting to an age where she desperately needs a woman's guidance. What are you going to say when she asks you about—about boys, for example?"

Matt brightened. "I'll tell her the truth—not one of them can be trusted."

Laura sniffed. "That will be helpful."

Matt glared at her. "I've forgot more about boys than you'll ever know."

"Probably," she said without offense. "But at least I admit I don't know it all. If—"

"That's enough!" John held up his hands. "Matt, look at the responses to Prince Charming's ad and pick one."

"The hell I will!"

"Do it for Jessica."

Matt stood there for a moment, frozen. Then with a groan, he reached inside the folder without even looking and pulled out a sheet of paper. Handing it to his grandfather, he tossed the file on the desk, whirled and strode out of the office.

His abrupt departure stunned Laura and she stared after him. "Of *course* Jessica needs a mother," she said self-righteously. "The poor little thing needs a role model, for heaven's sake."

John looked dubious. "I don't know, Laura. He was pretty steamed when he left."

"So? He won't be the first parent who has to make a tough choice to put his child first. It comes with the territory. I'm just afraid that if he won't go along with this, it'll break Jessica's heart and—"

"Hi, Grandpa." The bright little voice from the doorway brought John and Laura swinging around.

"Hi, Sugar." John waved Jessica in with a guilty expression on his face. "You just missed your father."

"That's okay." She glanced at Laura. "I just came to find out…uh…if…you know."

John nodded. "Laura knows and so does your dad. I just gave him the file with all the replies."

A flush of joy spread over the girl's face. "Did he

pick one?'' she asked breathlessly. ''Oh, Grandpa, did he?''

''Yes, but—''

''Let me see!''

Jessica flew to the desk, hand outstretched. Before John could react, she snatched the sheet of paper from him and began to read, '' 'Dear Prince Charming, My mama is nice and pretty. Please pick her, my daddy is—'' Her eyes went wide.

Laura smiled encouragement. ''Read the rest of it, honey. I think it was a wonderful thing for you to do for your father. Everyone in town's interested in how this turns out. Who's the letter from?''

Jessica glanced at her grandfather. He nodded gravely.

''It's from Zach G.,'' she said in a breathless voice, her gaze pinned on Laura.

''Zach G.'' Laura's smile slipped and she stared. ''But Zach G. is—'' She gasped. ''You don't mean—?''

Jessica looked down at the tips of her dirty sneakers. Her cut-off jean shorts weren't in much better condition, and her blue T-shirt was old and stretched out of shape. ''I helped him write it, Mrs. Laura,'' she admitted. ''I told him I was going to find a mother in the newspaper and he said he wanted a daddy, and could he look, too?''

Laura's stomach dropped with a sickening lurch. It was one thing for Matt's daughter to want a mother but quite another for Laura's son to long for a father. And *I'm a good* mother, too, she thought a bit wildly.

Then it occurred to her that Matt might be a really

good father and still not be able to provide all his child wanted and needed.

For what seemed an eternity, no one said a word. Then John said, "It could be worse, Laura. At least you know each other."

Laura groaned. "Know each other but don't—" She couldn't go on and say "Don't like each other" with Jessica's clear trusting gaze upon her.

"Still, you may have to put your money where your mouth is." John filled in the blanks.

She had no idea what he was talking about. "Such as?"

"You said a bunch of stuff about making tough choices—something like that."

"Yes, but—"

"If it was a wonderful thing for Jessica to do for her father, it's just as wonderful for a son to do for his mother," John pointed out. "And even more so because he's younger."

"Yes, but—"

"I *already* like you," Jessica said earnestly. "I bet you're already a pretty good mother. Zach likes you, anyway."

Laura felt herself melting as she usually did when she was around this little girl. "I like to think I'm a good mother," she said, "but I'm afraid your father will have to choose someone else. I'm just not looking for a husband, Jessica."

"That's the good part!" Jessica came to stand before Laura's chair. The blue eyes, exactly like her father's, glowed with determination. "You don't have to look because me 'n' Zach did all the work!"

Laura tried for a light laugh but it came out more like a groan. "You don't understand, honey. A newspaper ad isn't the way people get together."

John said, "You were all for it when it was just Matt and some stranger."

"That was different." She chewed on her lower lip.

"Why?" Jessica's excitement appeared to be somewhat dampened. "Zach said you like kids and dogs so I guess you just don't like me." Crystal tears trembled on her long lashes.

"Oh, honey, I like you very much." And Laura pulled the little girl into her arms, knowing she was lost, completely lost.

CHAPTER FIVE

WHEN Matt got home from the construction site after seven o'clock that night, his grandfather had already relieved the baby-sitter and he and Jessica were eating popcorn and watching a Disney tape. Tired and disgruntled from a long and unsettling day, Matt grunted a greeting and plunged through the family room, intent upon drowning his woes in a hot shower.

Standing beneath the stinging spray, he closed his eyes and tried to relax. The subdivision project was going just fine; construction of the new business park was going just fine; the only thing that *wasn't* going just fine was Laura Gilliam's family room. But to paraphrase one of Jessica's favorite cartoon characters, he had to admit that he "knew the job was dangerous when he took it."

Everything about Laura Gilliam, from her beauty to her utter conviction that she was always right, was dangerous, at least to his peace of mind. If he ever got that family room finished, he was going to run as far and as fast from the woman as he could possibly manage.

But before he could do that, he had to deal with this Prince Charming debacle. If only he'd kept his big mouth shut, perhaps he could have handled it quietly and diplomatically. Instead he'd missed no opportunity to heap scorn upon the mystery man's head—his own head, as it had turned out.

Toweling his wet hair, he tossed on a pair of shorts and a T-shirt and walked barefoot to the family room. They'd turned off the video and were waiting for him. He didn't like the avid expression on his daughter's face one little bit.

He tossed the damp towel on the back of his favorite leather reclining chair. "You already have dinner, squirt?"

"Grandpa bought me a hamburger."

"Great. In that case, I'll hit the leftover Chinese food." He turned toward the kitchen.

"Hold it, boy."

Matt wanted to groan but didn't. Slowly he turned back, pasting an insincere smile on his mouth. "What's on your mind, Grandpa?"

"You are, Prince Charming."

This time, Matt really did groan. "Okay, you've had your little joke. Let's just forget all that."

"Daddy!" Jessica looked offended. "We can't forget it. You've got to go out on dates and stuff."

"Yeah," John agreed. "Gotta see if that glass slipper fits." He laughed and Jessica added her giggles.

Matt did *not* laugh. "Don't you think this has gone far enough?" he asked plaintively. "I don't have time for..." His words trailed off, for Jessica suddenly looked on the verge of tears.

"You don't even know who got picked," she said in an accusing tone.

He sighed. "It doesn't matter, honey."

"It matters to me, Daddy."

Her gaze, level and filled with hope, locked with his. His stomach clenched and love welled up to choke him. He would do anything for his daughter.

Including pretend to give serious consideration to some woman who had so little respect for herself that she'd answer a blind ad in the newspaper?

"Daddy," she pleaded, "*please,* for me? Go out with this lady and fall in love and get married, okay?"

He had to laugh; as if that was all it took. "Jessica, honey—"

"How do you know if you don't try? That's what you always say to me." Her voice became low and pompous. "Jessica, eat those vegetables. How do you know you don't like them if you don't try?"

John grinned. "She's got you, boy."

And with a deep sigh, Matt realized that she did, indeed, "have him." Well, how much harm could it do to take out some strange woman on a single date? If that would make Jessica happy…

"Okay," he gave in, "but only—"

"Daddy!" She launched herself into his arms. "I'm so happy."

Her happiness was his. He hugged his little girl to him. "So who is this Cinderella I'm supposed to romance?"

Jessica leaned back in his arms so she could look up into his face, her own suffused with happiness. "Didn't we tell you?" she asked. "It's Mrs. Laura, Zach's mother!"

The first thing that occurred to Matt was that he'd completely misjudged Laura. The fact that she'd responded to the ad boggled his mind. And she'd always acted so cool!

First moment he had alone, he called her, all indignant and ready to raise hell. Her soft "Hello?" threw him before he even got started.

Her voice on the phone was light and filled with anticipation, as if she'd been waiting all day for just this particular call. Of course, she used the phone a great deal in her work so Matt supposed it was a professional thing. It sure as hell wasn't anything personal about *him*.

"It's Matt, Laura."

Even in the ensuing silence, he could hear charm give way to caution.

Finally she said, "Hello, Matt. I didn't expect to hear from you quite so soon."

"But you did expect to hear from me."

"Well, yes."

"So what are we going to do about this Prince Charming fiasco?"

"What do you want to do about it?"

"Avoid breaking my daughter's heart."

"Ditto for my son."

Matt frowned at the telephone. "What's Zach got to do with this?"

Another silence. Then she said, "You didn't actually read the letter, did you."

"No, but I was surprised you'd answered that ad after—"

"I didn't!"

He could hear her angry intake of breath over the wire. "Then what happened?"

"Zach answered the Prince Charming ad, with a little help from Jessica. A-apparently—" Her tone became ragged. "Apparently Zach wants a father as much as Jessica wants a mother."

"I'm sorry," he said, instantly contrite because he'd thought for a single instant that she'd answer a lonely hearts ad. Besides, he knew too well the questions she was asking herself: where did I go wrong? Why am I not enough for my child? How can I remedy this situation?

"Yes, well—" He could almost see her pulling herself together. "That's neither here nor there. The question is, where do we go from here?"

"I've been thinking about that," he admitted. "Look, a date or two won't kill us, right?"

The wait for her answer was not flattering. "Probably...not."

"Then let's do it for the kids. All it'll cost us is a little time."

"I suppose you're right."

"Then what do you want to do? I could take everyone out to dinner tomorrow night."

"I have a better idea. How about..." Her voice trailed off as if she couldn't bring herself to actually cooperate with him.

"Go ahead, Laura, say it. Don't make this a bigger deal than it is. It isn't brain surgery, it's one lousy date."

"Keep talking like that and it won't be!"

"Sorry. I've had a hard day."

"So who hasn't? Okay, we may as well get this over with as quick as we can. How about you and

Jessica come to dinner here tomorrow night, six o'clock.''

"Six! I usually work later than that.''

"The children shouldn't have to wait for their dinner to accommodate your schedule.''

"Yeah, okay, I suppose," he muttered ungraciously. "But why your house?" He was thinking, *your turf!*

"Because I'm not ready to start gossip by appearing in public with you," she said flatly, without any attempt to soften that potential blow to his ego.

"Okay, your house, tomorrow, six o'clock. We'll be there.''

"Fine.'' She hung up.

For a moment he glared at the telephone. Then he reminded himself that at least he'd get a home-cooked meal out of it.

Laura was gratified at the prompt arrival of Matt and Jessica at six o'clock the following evening. Jessica and Zach beamed at each other as if they were the two happiest kids in the world. Matt looked annoyed and Laura supposed she must look dubious at best.

"Please come in," she invited as formally as if they were strangers.

"Thank you," Matt replied just as formally.

Zach grabbed Matt's hand. "So when you and Mama getting married?" he asked in his little-boy voice.

Matt and Laura stared at each other, stricken. Jessica came to the rescue.

"You shouldn't ask a question like that," she

scolded the little boy. "They've got to go out at least two or three times before they get married."

"Oh," he said, obviously confused by her counsel. "But I want a daddy now."

Matt laughed, and it broke at least part of the tension. "You're a lot like your mother," he told the small boy. "You want what you want when you want it."

Zach said, "Uh-huh," in a "doesn't everyone?" tone. "Com' on, Jess, let's go see Lucy."

"Lucy?" Matt inquired.

"My cat."

"I love cats! I love dogs, too" Still holding his hand, Jessica allowed the little boy to lead her from the room. "I've got a dog named Fluffy. You'll like her—"

They were alone. Laura licked her lips and tried to avoid looking at him. "Uh…this is awkward, but if we all try I'm sure we can get through one evening. The children are so happy."

"Yeah, but what happens when they realize nothing's gonna come of this?"

She sighed. "I've thought about that. But if we give them no real reason to hope…" She turned toward the kitchen and he followed. "…and if we're very careful not to show anything except friendship—"

"Laura," he said, "we've never been friends. Best we've ever managed was acquaintances."

"True, but now we've got to do better than that." She stopped in front of the refrigerator. "I think it's important, though, that we not let our children get too attached to someone who's—excuse me for being blunt, but someone who's just passing through.''

"Yeah, you're right about that. When they realize this isn't going to work out, we don't want them to be hurt.''

"That's right. We can let them down easy. Of course, I really like Jessica a lot, and even after this charade is over I'd like to be her friend…at least until you find her a real mother.''

"That's not going to happen anytime soon," he said grimly. "I feel the same about Zach. He's a great kid but I'll try not to encourage him.''

"I'd appreciate that. Would you like a beer?''

"Yeah, thanks. Will you join me?''

"I'll have a glass of wine.'' She pulled the wine bottle and a can of beer from the refrigerator and closed the door.

"I'll open the wine for you.'' He took the bottle from her, their fingers brushing.

She pulled back quickly, her breathing just a little faster. "The corkscrew is in that top drawer.''

"Must be your junk drawer," he said, opening it. "Everyone has a few of those.''

"*I* don't.''

He'd just found that out. He'd never seen such a neat drawer in his life. Everything fit perfectly into its own little compartment.

While he opened the wine, she brought a stemmed glass and a stein and stood waiting patiently. Unfortunately, the kids chose that moment to come dashing into the room. They stopped short at sight of their parents, doing for each other things they normally did for themselves.

Jessica's smile struck terror into Laura's heart. The little girl was already reading volumes into the most innocent act. But when Matt poured the wine, then met Laura's thanks with a long, steady gaze, her stomach did a little flip-flop. She poured his beer and he lifted it in a salute.

"Cheers," he said. "To us—may we survive our children's manipulations."

Laura said, "Amen!" and drank.

"We'll eat in the dining room," Laura announced. "Would you like to help me set the table, Jessica?"

Matt and young Zach exchanged frowning glances and Matt figured they were of one mind on this subject. "Couldn't we eat here in the kitchen?" he asked plaintively.

"Certainly not." Laura looked shocked he'd suggest it. "The kitchen's not for company."

"Don't think of us as company," Matt urged. "Think of us as..."

"As what?" She arched one slender brow.

"Forget it," he muttered. "I guess we *are* company after all."

Jessica gave him an exasperated glance. "Are we using real napkins?" she wanted to know.

"We use napkins at home," Matt said. "You make us sound like pigs, Jess."

"I mean *real* napkins. We use paper napkins at home."

Laura smiled. She really was extraordinarily beautiful when she smiled. "Zach and I often use paper napkins but we'll use my good linen napkins today," she said. "That's because it's special to have you here, Jessica."

"And Daddy," she added quickly.

"And Daddy." Laura gave Matt an oblique glance into which he could read nothing. "We'll use the good china, too."

Zach gave a little-boy groan. When he saw Matt looking at him, he muttered, "I got in trouble for breaking one of Mama's good plates."

Laura and Jessica had gone into the dining room so Matt felt safe in whispering, "Don't worry, Zach, that's part of growing up. I still break plates sometimes but now I don't get into trouble for it—much."

The little boy looked delighted. "Really?"

"Really what?" Laura asked, reentering the kitchen.

"Nothing," Zach said quickly, exchanging a conspiratorial glance with Matt. "What's for dinner, Mama?"

"Cornish game hens," Laura said with evident satisfaction. "And a chocolate layer torte."

"Ugh," Zach said.

"Zachery Gilliam!" Laura faced her recalcitrant son with hands on hips. "We'll have none of that."

"But I like *big* chickens!"

Jessica asked, "What's a Cornish gang hen?"

"That's *game* hen, honey." Laura turned on the burner beneath a pan already on the stove. "It's like a small chicken and you get a whole one just for yourself."

Jessica's eyes went wide. "A *whole chicken* just for me? What's wrong with that, Zach?"

Matt, who honestly couldn't abide those sorry excuses for chickens, nudged the little boy on the shoulder. "Buck up, kid," he said. "Growing up means learning to eat what women put in front of you without gagging. It's a guy thing."

"Matthew!" Laura gave him a frosty look that soon dissolved into a smile. "Don't put ideas like that into his head."

"The sooner he learns, the happier he'll be." Matt winked at Zach. "And men have to learn to use their napkins instead of dropping them on the floor, and to eat with a fork instead of their fingers and to eat their soup with a spoon instead of drinking out of a bowl."

Zach burst into peals of laughter. "Sometimes Mama puts my soup in a cup and I drink it!" he shouted.

"If it's in a cup, you can get away with that," Matt conceded.

"At least I like that chocolate stuff," Zach grumbled.

Matt didn't. He never put chocolate into his mouth if he could avoid it. Somehow the general fascination with all things chocolate had entirely passed him by. He'd much rather have had one of Laura's apple pies. Made his mouth water, just thinking about it.

"Time to wash up," Laura told the children. "Matt, will you see that they do a good job?"

"Sure," he agreed, "but who's gonna see that *I* do a good job?"

Amid much laughing and giggling, he pursued the duo down the hall toward the bathroom.

Dinner, Laura thought, went just fine.

Jessica, especially, seemed to enjoy herself, handling the silver and china with something akin to reverence and using her very best manners. Zach, on the other hand, ate with sloppy disregard until a quiet word from Matt reminded him that even guys needed manners. After that, he ate with more decorum than Laura had seen from him in some time.

At first, she'd been annoyed when Matt had spoken so teasingly about "learning to eat what women put in front of you without gagging." But then she'd realized it was an effort on Matt's part to make contact with the boy. Still, she wasn't too crazy about her six-year-old son hearing about "guy things."

Jessica placed her spoon carefully on her dessert plate. "Umm!" she rolled her eyes ecstatically. "That chocolate stuff—"

"It's a torte, dear."

"That chocolate torte is the best. I wish I could learn to cook but Daddy—"

"No daddy-knocking," Matt put in quickly. "I taught you to make chocolate pudding, didn't I?"

"Yeah," Jessica agreed scornfully, "but just the kind you put in a bowl with milk and beat up for five minutes."

"You've got to crawl before you can walk," Matt retorted, poking around at the chocolate mass on his plate. He didn't actually seem to be eating much of it.

"I can't even bake cookies," Jessica groused.

"I could teach you," Laura said hesitantly, "that is, if it's all right with your father."

"Sure," he said, "whatever." He put his fork down on his plate.

Laura frowned. "Is something wrong with your dessert?"

"Daddy hates chocolate," Jessica announced.

"Really?"

He gave his daughter a quelling glance. "I don't exactly *hate* chocolate. I just don't love it."

"Well," Laura said, trying not to let him get to her, "that's not a guy thing because lots of guys really like chocolate."

He raised his brows. "I've got no quarrel with that."

"Next you'll be telling me you meant all those remarks you made about game hens," she said lightly.

"Actually..." He looked genuinely regretful. "I like my chickens bigger, not smaller."

"Like turkeys!" Zach cried.

"Or ducks," Matt agreed.

"Or eagles!"

"Zach, nobody eats eagles," Matt said. "They're an endangered species or something. You could be thrown in jail for eating an eagle."

Zach responded with uproarious laughter. "*You'd* go to jail," he exclaimed. "Nobody puts little kids in jail."

"You got me there, partner."

Laura, watching the exchange, felt a warm glow

inside. She'd never heard such genuine laughter at her dinner table. She wasn't happy to learn that Matt didn't appreciate her gourmet cooking but she'd trade that kind of approval for the sound of her child's laughter any day.

Then Jessica caught her glance and silently mouthed the word, "Men!"

The girl was obviously a quick study.

"Hate to eat and run," Matt announced, "but—"

"Not a chance."

He blinked. "Are you going to hold me hostage or what?"

"Yes." She grinned and he felt the warmth of it run through him like a lightning bolt. "You can go after you help me with the dishes."

"You're kidding."

"No, I'm not."

"Dishwasher broken? I could probably fix it for you."

"The dishwasher is just fine, but I'm not about to put china and crystal and silver in it." Picking up the stack of dishes she'd amassed while they spoke, she rose and carried it toward the kitchen.

He picked up a couple of serving bowls and followed her. "I told you we should eat in the kitchen," he complained. "Paper plates and plastic forks—that's my style."

She put the dishes on the counter and turned so unexpectedly that he walked right into her. With arms extended to hold a dish in each hand, she was effectively trapped in an embrace that wasn't quite an embrace at all.

But her thighs pressed against his, and her breasts nearly touched his chest. He sucked in a quick breath, thinking that he'd never realized how smooth and glowing her skin was, how deep the womanly knowledge in her eyes, how soft and inviting her lips....

Which moved when she said breathlessly, "I'm sorry you didn't like the menu. I'm actually a decent cook."

"I know you are. I didn't intend to say anything."

"If I had known I could have..." She licked those luscious lips.

He swayed a hair closer. "I'm a steak and potatoes kind of guy."

"I'm a gourmet cook."

"I'm a beer and potato chips kind of guy."

"I'm a connoisseur of fine w-wines."

"I say po-*tay*-toe."

"And I say po-*tah*—"

He ended the conversation by lowering his lips and brushing them lightly across hers. Her mouth felt every bit as soft as it looked. She stood as still as a beautiful statue, but somehow he felt that inside her, something was softening, warming—

He sucked in a deep breath, aware that she smelled of flowers and spring rain. For the first time in memory, he felt awkward as a schoolboy. He wanted to touch her, to cup his hands beneath her breasts and bury his face in that silken mass of blond hair.

He wanted to make love to—

"Hey, Laura, I dropped by to tell you—holy cow! What's going on here?"

Laura sprang sideways and out of his reach, nearly knocking a dish out of his hand in the process. "Katy! What are you doing here?"

"I just told you," Katy drawled. "Howdy, Matthew. Would you care to jump in here and tell me what *you're* doing here?"

Matt placed the dishes on the counter. His heart raced and his gut clenched in unexpected reaction to what had nearly happened. If Katy hadn't arrived when she did— He almost snarled at her. "I don't think that's any of your business, Katy."

"Getting testy, are we?" She pulled out a kitchen chair and plunked herself down in it. All of a sudden her eyes widened in understanding. "I get it, you're trying each other out because of the Prince Charming thing."

"Trying each other out!" Laura stared at her friend, her expression appalled.

Katy shrugged. "Whatever." Her eyes twinkled with mischief. "So how was it? The old spark still there?"

"What old spark?" Matt wanted to know.

"Hey, this is Katy you're talking to! Aren't you the Matthew Reynolds who came to me right after Laura came to town, asking all kinds of questions about the hot new life-styles editor?"

Damn, he'd forgotten about that. "I didn't know her then," he muttered. "You can't call that a spark."

"And you, Laura—didn't you come back from a chamber of commerce luncheon just a few weeks after you got here and ask who the studly president was?''

Laura's mouth fell open. ''I have never used the word *studly* to describe anyone or anything in my entire life.''

''But that's what you meant,'' Katy said airily. ''Maybe you just said cute or drop-dead gorgeous or something dull like that, but you meant studly, all right.''

Katy might be obnoxious but it was worth putting up with her to see the soft color sweep up Laura's throat and across her cheeks. Matt felt a swell of pride that she'd noticed him enough to inquire.

''And now,'' Katy said, ''I walk in here and find you two making out in the kitchen—''

''Katy, that's enough.'' Laura glared at her friend. ''I must insist that you not go around repeating anything you saw here—in fact, I don't even want anyone in town to know that Matt's *been* here. We're doing this for the children, that's all. Promise you won't say a word.''

''I promise.''

Laura blinked in surprise. ''Well, that was easy.''

''Sure.'' Katy laughed. ''Because I don't *have* to say a word. Everyone in town knows you two are here together and they're rooting for you.''

CHAPTER SIX

APRIL FORBES knew.

She greeted Laura the next morning with a big smile and a cheerful, "So how's the big romance with Prince Charming coming along?"

Laura's stomach tightened and she stopped short, caught completely by surprise. How could the Rawhide grapevine travel so fast?

She took a deep breath to steady herself. "There's no big romance," she said, "and how did *you* hear about it?"

April blinked. "I don't actually remember who told me." She shrugged. "I thought everybody knew."

"Well, everybody *doesn't* so I'd appreciate it if you'd refrain from further gossip."

"Gosh, Laura." April's grandmotherly face wrinkled with remorse. "I didn't mean any harm. I'm happy that you and Matt—"

"There is no me and Matt," Laura interrupted. "We're just working together to try to appease the kids—his daughter and my son. You do know that Jessica placed the ad?"

"Of course." April brightened. "Tell you what, if anyone brings it up, I'll just—"

"*Please* don't say a word! You'll have to forgive me for being cross but I don't like to think that people are talking about me. It makes me very uneasy."

April nodded sympathetically. "I see your point but it's kind of hopeless, trying to keep things quiet in a small town like Rawhide. When everybody knows everybody, nothing's sacred."

Laura sighed. "You're probably right, but I can try."

In the cubbyhole in the newsroom that she called an office, she tossed her purse on a neat desk and slumped into her chair. She'd barely slept the previous night, instead spending it tossing and turning and remembering the power of Matt's kiss. If Katy hadn't shown up at the worst possible moment—

Or maybe Katy had shown up at the *best* moment, for it was impossible to know what might have happened. The truth was, Laura had enjoyed the entire evening, even if Matt hadn't enjoyed the menu.

She reached over to switch on her computer and stared unseeing at the flickering monitor as it went through various screens to reach her desktop. She could cook meat and potatoes; she could cook *anything*. The question was, did she want to?

Not if you're smart, a little voice inside her head warned. You and Matt are oil and water—no, that's not right, because the two of you together are a potentially combustible combination. He makes you feel things you haven't felt since—

"He does not," she muttered aloud.

"Who doesn't what?"

Laura looked up in surprise to find Katy standing before the desk, grinning.

"Nothing," Laura muttered. "Is there something I can do for you, Katy?"

"Ohh, you're cross today. Didn't you sleep well?"

"I slept great. But at the moment, I have a lot of work to do, so if you don't—"

"I do," Katy said hastily. "Want to do lunch? I'll be finished by twelve-thirty and I thought we could go to the Rawhide Café and snag a few of those great French fries."

"Salad bar," Laura corrected.

Katy laughed. "To each her own. Is it a date?"

Laura consulted an overflowing appointment book always kept open on her desk. "I have to get my pages in by eleven, then I've got an eleven-thirty appointment with the president of the Rawhide Ladies' Club about some big national award they just received. Okay, lunch will work. I'll have plenty of time to meet you."

Katy gave a thumbs-up. "Great." She waved and turned away. "I'll see you at twelve-thirty, then."

Laura nodded and picked up the dummy sheets laying on her desk. She wasn't looking forward to going out in public if everyone was going to be whispering and pointing, but she'd have to face it sooner or later.

She called up the menu of the day's stories on her computer, working automatically. She might as well be brave, she consoled herself. Besides, she could very well be stressing about nothing. Probably no one knew or even cared about the Prince Charming debacle except employees of the Rawhide *Review*.

It took her about thirty seconds after her arrival at the Rawhide Ladies Clubhouse to realize how misplaced her optimism had been. Amanda Willy, a lively and

beautiful senior citizen, rushed forward with outstretched hands and a big smile.

"How wonderful of you to come, Laura," she said.

"How wonderful that your club has received such
an impressive award," Laura countered pleasantly.

"Well, while we're talking about wonderful things,
how wonderful that you've found your very own
Prince Charming. Matthew is a fine young man. He
deserves a wonderful girl like you."

Struck nearly speechless, Laura tried to stammer
out a denial which Amanda waved airily away.

"We've all heard about it, dear," she said serenely,
"and I can't tell you how delighted we are. I, per-
sonally, have been quite concerned about Matt. He's
never been the same since his wife's death." She
peered at Laura with bright, curious eyes, but also
with sympathy. "You're a widow, I believe someone
mentioned."

"That's right."

"In that case, I'm sure you can appreciate how
much the loss of a loved one can affect a body."
Amanda gestured for Laura to precede her. "I thought
we could talk in the club lounge, dear. I've made
coffee...." Still chatting cheerfully, she followed
Laura toward the back of the large meeting room.

Laura tried to concentrate but she was distracted by
new possibilities. She'd supposed Matt had always
been exactly as she'd found him: easy-go-lucky, self-
centered and elusive. The thought that he might have
been different once disturbed her for some reason.

She wanted to ask Amanda to elaborate but bit her
tongue. Katy could tell her what she needed to know

without encouraging still more gossip. Laura sat down on the easy chair Amanda indicated and pulled out a pen and a reporter's notebook.

"So tell me," she began, once coffee had been served, "what did the Rawhide Ladies Club do to earn such an honor?"

But she was thinking about Matt...again.

The interview ended early so Laura decided to stop by the dry cleaners on her way to the Rawhide Café. There the girl behind the counter grinned and winked.

"So how are you getting along with Prince Charming?" she inquired. "I thought it was *so* romantic, putting an ad in the paper like that and all. And when it turned out to be Matt Reynolds—wow! You could have knocked me over with a feather."

Laura would have *liked* to knock the chattering girl over with a feather but good sense prevailed. Instead she paid for her silk blouse, smiled weakly and escaped.

She pulled up before the Rawhide Café at twelve-twenty. Since she didn't see Katy's car, she dashed inside the Grab 'n' Go convenience store next door to pick up a six-pack of water for the office.

The man behind the counter grinned as he rang up the sale. "So how's it goin' with Prince Charming?" he inquired. "Heh-heh, I guess that makes you Cinderella, Laura."

What it made her was desperate to avoid further inquiries into her personal life. Didn't these people have anything better to think about? To gossip about?

Inside the crowded Rawhide Café, she spotted Katy

just seating herself—in a dark corner, thank heaven. Laura rushed to join her friend, weaving through the round tables and responding absently to those who greeted her. Did she only imagine it or were many of them whispering behind their hands? And if so, who were they talking about—as if she didn't know.

"You look stressed," Katy observed. "What's up?"

Laura shrugged and sat down. Unfolding a paper napkin, she dropped it into her lap. "You were right—the whole town's talking. I'm getting the third degree everywhere I go."

"Just be cool and it'll all blow over," Katy advised.

"The question is, *when?*"

"When you and Matt are married and have a couple of kids." Katy smiled.

She meant it as a joke, but Laura felt a disconcerting thrill all the way to her toes. *Making kids with Matt* was not something she wanted to think about. ·

"Speaking of whom—"

Katy glanced significantly toward the front of the busy café. Laura's gaze automatically followed. She spotted Matt at once, standing just inside the door and looking around for an empty table which did not exist.

Katy raised an arm and waved to catch his attention.

Laura frowned. "Oh, Katy, don't."

Katy looked astonished. "It's the least we can do, especially considering this crowd," she said reasonably. "Besides, it would look funny if Cinderella and Prince Charming didn't dine at the same table."

"*Dine* is much too elegant for what we do at the Rawhide Café," Laura said, watching the tall man walk toward them. Before he even reached the table, she thought she saw in Matt the same reluctance that was straining her nerves.

Life was suddenly getting very complicated.

To a self-contained and well-organized woman like Laura Gilliam, this was not a good thing.

Matt didn't want to sit at Laura's table. Just the sight of her reminded him of the kiss they'd shared last night, and he *sure* didn't want to be reminded of that. But with Katy sitting there beaming at them both with that I-know-your-secret look on her face, how was he going to think of anything else?

This was ridiculous. Even for the sake of the children, he didn't see how he could go on with this charade much longer.

But every time he looked at Laura, he thought about how sweet her lips had felt beneath his...how quietly she'd stood there in his arms...how beautiful she'd looked—

"*Matt!* Do you plan to eat or just sit there staring at Laura? The waitress would like your order."

Matt felt like an idiot. "Burger and fries," he said quickly. "And a tall glass of iced tea."

"Got it, Prince Charming." The waitress winked and then sashayed away.

And everybody at the small table just sat there, waiting for who-knew-what to happen.

Nothing happened, thank heaven—if you could call the covert glances of dozens of diners nothing. Laura could barely force down her salad. Matt hardly said a word, which would have been terribly awkward if Katy hadn't kept up a running commentary.

Laura ate quickly, eager to escape. She was the first one finished, which wasn't too surprising, considering she didn't even eat half of the food she'd anxiously piled on her plate at the salad bar. Putting down her fork, she reached for her shoulder bag on the floor near her feet.

"I don't mean to rush but I've got a ton of work to do this afternoon." She dropped a ten dollar bill on the table. "If you'll excuse me—"

Matt reached out to touch her arm, halting her flight. It took all her willpower not to flinch and then to stand there and try to listen with the light pressure of his fingers still on her flesh.

"I really need to talk to you." He let his hand drop back onto the table. "Is it all right if Jessica and I drop by tonight after dinner? It won't take long."

"I—why, I suppose."

"About seven," he said urgently. "I wouldn't ask if it wasn't important."

That could be taken any number of ways. "I suppose it will be all right," Laura said with a calm that belied the butterflies in her stomach. "I'll expect you at seven, then."

"Thanks," he said. "I appreciate it."

Like she had a choice.

Dylan entered as Katy was leaving, making his way to Matt's table and sitting down. He ordered a cup of coffee, then broke his friend's brooding silence. "What's the matter? Is this all getting a little too real for you?"

His question jolted Matt. "What'a ya mean, too real?"

"It started as kind of a joke—this whole Prince Charming thing. Laura. Zachery, the whole package. Now it's like taking over your whole life."

"No way." Matt straightened in his chair. "You know damned good and well that I am *not* looking for a wife."

"Maybe you need one." Dylan looked thoughtful. "And maybe Laura's the one you need."

Matt saw red. "That's a helluva thing to say to me. Laura doesn't even like me. I didn't place that ad anyway, Jess did—"

Dylan cut in. "You're squirming, buddy."

"I'm *not* squirming." Matt spoke in a surly tone, squirming in his chair. He caught himself and sat up straight and stiff. "I was willing to go along with this Prince Charming thing for a little while to let Jessica figure out on her own that what she wants just ain't gonna happen. I didn't count on becoming the hot topic in town, though."

"Like you think Laura did?" Dylan shook his head, his expression amused. "The funny thing is…"

"What?"

"On the face of it, you two are the perfect match."

Matt glared at Dylan with disbelief. "Get outta here!"

"I mean it. On top of that, I'm seeing…changes in you."

"Jeez, are you supposed to be my friend or what? I'd sooner wrestle a bear than get tangled up with another 'good woman.'"

"You're already tangled up with one. Admit it— you've got it bad for the luscious Laura."

After that, Matt couldn't get away fast enough. On the drive to the construction site, he found himself lost in memories. His wife had certainly been a good woman. Their marriage had been far from perfect, and when she died his grief had been mixed with guilt. He wasn't sure how he'd have handled it if he hadn't had little Jessica to think of. He didn't ever intend to go through that kind of agony again.

It *was* dangerous to get tangled up with a good woman, dangerous on so many different levels that it made a man's head spin.

And there was not a single doubt in his mind that Laura was, indeed, a good woman.

By the time seven o'clock rolled around, Laura was a nervous wreck. She couldn't imagine any reason Matt would want to talk to her except to call off this whole silly Prince Charming business. And while she almost desperately hoped he'd come up with a way to do that without traumatizing the children, she couldn't help feeling the tiniest little shaft of resentment.

One "date" with her and he was ready to run for the hills! So he didn't like Cornish game hens or chocolate, she'd still gone out of her way to be a good hostess and yet—

She pulled such thoughts up short, a wry smile tugging at her mouth. Whatever he had to say wasn't *personal,* after all. She turned back to the cake she was making. Nothing like a good bout of baking to take her mind off—

A knock on the kitchen door sent her bolting around. But when she went to answer, she found Zach's baby-sitter, Abby Royce, standing there smiling.

"I think I left my book here," she said. "It's a romance and I was just getting to the good part when Zach asked to go to the park."

"I think it's in living room," Laura said. "Looks good. Can I borrow it when you're finished?"

"Sure!" Abby dashed out, returning in a flash carrying a paperback book with a bright happy cover. Instead of leaving, she loitered.

"Zach told me how much fun you and Matt had last night," she offered slyly.

"Matt and me? I thought *Zach* was the one having fun—and Jessica, too, of course."

"Well, sure, that's what he said—everybody had fun. But Matt's so *studly!*" Abby sighed deeply. "He's smart, too, owns his own construction company and all. You could do a whole lot worse, Laura."

"Abby, dear," Laura said sweetly, "there is nothing between me and Matt Reynolds. We—we're just trying to let the children spend a little time together." Yeah, anybody would believe that: a nine-year-old girl and a six-year-old boy, best friends? Gotta do better than that, Laura!

Abby laughed. "Com' on, I know all about that

Prince Charming stuff. What I didn't hear around town, Zach told me—and I wasn't pumping him for information, either,'' she added hastily. ''He's just so happy about it that he can't stop talking. He really wants a daddy bad.''

Laura sighed. ''I know.'' But she hadn't known *how* bad until very recently. She measured milk and oil and broke two eggs on top of the flour and other dry ingredients in the large mixer bowl. ''He'll get over it, though,'' she added. He'll have to.

''Maybe he won't have to get over it,'' Abby suggested helpfully. ''If you and Matt end up getting married—''

''We are *not* going to end up getting married. Please don't go around saying that, Abby.''

''Okay, okay, whatever.'' The girl crossed to the kitchen door and threw it open. ''But you never know what's going to—eek!''

Matt and Jessica stood on the small back porch, his fist raised to knock.

''Hi, Mr. Reynolds,'' Abby gushed. ''Hi, Jessica.''

''Yeah, right.'' Matt was all business. He dug around in his pocket. ''Abby, I saw the Jolly Roger truck coming down this street. Why don't you take the kids and get ice cream cones for the lot of you?''

''Sure! Where's Zach—oh, there you are,'' she added, for the boy, who'd been playing in the fenced front yard, had come running up to grab Jessica's hand. ''Ice cream for all! Let's go, kids!''

They took off in a rush, the teenage Abby apparently as excited at the prospect as the younger kids.

Laura smiled after them, not eager to face whatever Matt was about to drop on her.

He walked inside and closed the door. He didn't smile. Nervously, Laura poked at the bowl of cake mix with a rubber spatula.

She heard his footsteps as he approached, and then his low voice almost in her ear. "Have you been getting as much flak around town as I have?"

"Flak?"

"Comments. Remarks. Cracks."

"You mean…about us? The Prince Charming thing…" She turned to face him at last and was sorry she had. He looked so grimly determined—so grimly attractive.

"That's right," he said, "the Prince Charming thing." He heaved a heavy sigh. "I can't go anywhere without catching it. I got a haircut and the barber started in on me. Hell, I was afraid to tell him to mind his own business for fear he'd cut off my ear. I went to the hardware store and the clerk wanted to know if we'd set a date yet. I stopped at the fried chicken store on my way home from work—"

"You fed that child greasy fried chicken for dinner? Really, Matt!"

"Once in a while, that's all." He looked defensive.

"I'm sorry," she apologized. "I jumped to conclusions, I guess. I'm…a little edgy tonight."

"Yeah, well, that's more like it." He seemed somewhat mollified. "Fried chicken isn't all Jess eats. Sometimes I feed her fast-food hamburgers, or frozen dinners from the super market."

Laura groaned and shook her head helplessly but

didn't pursue it. This was *not* her business. "And your point is?"

"That I'm currently the topic of every joke in town. Frankly, I don't like it."

Her temper flared. "You think I do? I go out on an interview but first I have to answer questions about my perceived love life. I pick up dry cleaning and it's more of the same. I go into the Grab 'n' Go—" She ran out of steam, finishing, "I guess you get the picture."

He nodded glumly. "I've been thinking that…well, that it's time we cut our losses and call this whole thing off before it gets entirely out of hand."

While she stood there trying to digest the fact that he'd really said exactly what she'd wanted to hear and wondering why there was no accompanying leap of joy, he noticed the batter in the mixer bowl.

"What are you making?"

"A cake." Okay, they'd reached a decision. Their little deception was over. It might take the town a few days to get used to the idea but—

"What kind?"

"Spice."—but once they did, life could get back to normal. Nice, safe, boring normal.

"Mind if I have a taste?"

Before she could protest, he dragged a forefinger through the creamy batter and popped it in his mouth and *her* mouth went dry. Then he licked his lips. "Umm. My mother used to make spice cakes. It's my favorite flavor."

Her laugher sounded abrupt even to her. "Better than chocolate, anyway."

"Anything's better than chocolate."

Outside on the street, the sounds of the Jolly Roger man drifted through the warm summer air: "Avast, me hearties—yo-ho-ho and a bar of ice cream!"

But the cry of the ice cream truck driver washed over her and was forgotten in a moment grown suddenly electric. Why was Matt staring at her that way? She lifted a hand hesitantly to her cheek. "Do I have a smudge on my cheek?"

He nodded. "A little bit of flour right…there."

He touched her face near the corner of her mouth, brushing away something she could not see. His touch took her breath away with it. She stared at him, her lips parted.

"So what do you think?" he asked in a low voice.

She licked her lips. "About what?"

"About calling off our little charade and letting Prince Charming die a graceful death."

She didn't want to think about Prince Charming dying *any* kind of death, but she didn't figure she was in a position to quibble over technicalities. "I suppose you're right. It is…very uncomfortable."

"Yeah, especially when none of it's true. If we really were involved, that would be something else."

"But we're not," she whispered. "And we never will be."

He stroked her cheek with calloused fingertips. "Of course not. We only got into this for our kids."

"They have to be our first priority," she agreed. She should step away from his hypnotic touch but her legs seemed somehow paralyzed. "We probably should tell them as soon as they finish their ice cream.''

''Tell them...what exactly?''

''That it just isn't working out.''

''All right.'' He slid his hand down her cheek and onto her shoulder, where he lingered. ''It'll be hard to convince them, unfortunately. Jessica's crazy about you.'' He didn't sound at all happy about that.

''And Zach follows you around like a puppy.''

''He's a good kid.''

For a moment longer they stared into each other's eyes. His were blue as the sky, deep as the ocean. She'd never realized how long his lashes were, how high his cheekbones beneath smooth brown skin...skin she suddenly longed to touch.

''Matt,'' she whispered, ''this is crazy.''

She didn't have to tell him what she meant by ''this.'' He knew. ''You're right,'' he agreed, his voice little more than a low rumble. ''We've got to avoid anything that might give the kids false hopes.''

Somehow she managed a nod. ''They're too little to realize that people don't get married just because it may seem like a good idea to someone else.''

''That's right. They're much too young to understand about love...about love between a man...and a woman...''

She didn't know who made the first move but suddenly she was crushed in his arms. When he leaned down, she lifted her mouth to meet his, instinctively angling her head in the opposite direction to accommodate his kiss.

She was instantly lost. Her heart slammed against

her ribs in alarm but still she opened her mouth to
his simply because she couldn't help herself. His fist
at the small of her back pressed her inexorably closer
to his aroused body. The possessiveness of the kiss
stunned her. It was as if she already belonged to him
and—

The kitchen door slammed open. For a stunned moment, nothing happened and then a little voice
shouted, ''Hey, Jessica, my mom's kissing your dad!
Hooray! We're getting married!''

CHAPTER SEVEN

LAURA ducked under his arm and scooted sideways as if escaping from the clutches of a doom. The look she gave him bespoke firing squads and lynching parties.

Like it's all *my* fault, Matt grumbled to himself. He'd come here to extricate them both from a difficult situation and instead they'd dug that hole deeper. Might as well face the music.

He turned toward the door with extreme reluctance. There stood the teenage baby-sitter with Jessica on one side and Zach on the other. Each held a chocolate-coated ice cream bar; each wore an enormous smile.

"Hooray!" Zach waved his ice cream in the air. "I gotta new daddy!"

"Not so fast!" Laura took a step toward the cluster of kids, her hand rising and her expression horrified.

Like it would be so bad for Matt to be a father to Zach? Matt pulled himself back to reality, scowling. "You kids are jumping to conclusions," he announced.

Zach executed a two-footed leap into the air. "I jump good," he cried. "Hooray, hooray!"

Laura groaned. "Stop saying hooray," she ordered him. "There's nothing to cheer about."

Jessica crossed the kitchen to take her father's

hand. "Daddy, I'm so happy," she exclaimed. "Gosh, I didn't know an ad in grandpa's newspaper would work *this* fast."

"Honey, you don't understand. We—"

But she'd already turned toward Laura. "Can I be flower girl?" she asked eagerly.

Zach frowned. "Is there a flower boy? Can I be it?"

"Silly!" Jessica laughed. "You can be the kid who carries the ring—what's that called?" She looked up questioningly at Laura.

"Ring bearer," Laura responded numbly. "But we don't need a ring bearer because—"

Abby interrupted. "I'll keep the guest book for you," she said eagerly. "I've only been to two weddings but I know how to do that. Oh, Laura, I'm so happy for you!"

"Stop, all of you!" Laura flung up her hands in a defensive gesture. "There's not going to be any wedding."

"Are you going to elope?" Abby looked puzzled by this possibility. "Do you think that's fair to the kids?" She gave the two youngsters a pitying glance.

"Absolutely not." Matt felt he had to take a stand here, too.

Abby sighed gratefully. "That's a relief. So maybe you just want a small wedding? My cousin Cynthia had a small wedding but she still had a flower girl and a ring bearer. You don't have to make a big deal of it if you want to—"

"Abby, will you hush?" Laura clenched trembling hands together at her waist. "You've all completely misunderstood the situation. Matt and I have no intention of getting married, soon or ever, big wedding or small, elopement or otherwise. Is that perfectly clear?''

The three stared at her—make that four. Matt wasn't particularly flattered by her vehemence.

''But—'' Abby frowned. ''If this isn't a serious relationship, why are you and Matt making out in your kitchen?''

Laura groaned. ''We weren't *making out,* as you put it. I had flour on my cheek and he—he...'' Her glance was a cry for help.

''I simply brushed it aside,'' he said indignantly, wondering who'd ever believe a story like that.

Not Abby, apparently. ''Like, what am I supposed to believe? You guys or my own eyes?''

''Exactly.'' Laura knelt to look into Zach's face. She didn't even flinch at the chocolate smears on his round cheeks, or the sticky white ice cream dripping down his arm. ''Honey, Jessica's daddy and I are just...'' She swallowed hard before going on. ''...friends. You and Jessica are the ones who want us to get married, not us.''

''Why not?'' Jessica asked in a tiny voice. All her exuberant happiness had disappeared and it cut her father to the quick to see it. ''Don't you like me, Mrs. Laura?''

''I like you very much.'' Laura pulled the little girl into her embrace with one arm, Zach with the other. Melting chocolate-coated ice cream smudged her white blouse but she didn't appear to notice. ''I just can't marry a man I don't love—'' She shot Matt a condemning glance. "—even a man as *wonderful* as your father."

Apparently only Matt knew how hard it was for her to say that word. But her explanation was enough to cause Jessica to brighten.

"You can *learn* to love him, I bet." She gave Laura a big hug, leaving a smear of chocolate on Laura's blond hair. "I'll try to be patient," she promised, "but I sure am in a hurry to have a mother around the house."

"It's not that simple, unfortunately."

"Sure it is. All you gotta do is *try*."

"But—"

"Go out on lots of dates," the little girl urged. "Have lots of fun and kiss and hug all the time."

Matt managed a wry laugh. "Is that how people fall in love? How did you figure that out, shrimp?"

"I go to movies," she said airily. "Ohh!" She jumped back, arms outstretched, and looked down at the ice cream staining the front of her T-shirt. Turning, she dropped the misshapen bar into the sink. "Daddy!"

"Yeah, I'll take you home and get you cleaned up."

"But first make another date," she instructed, turning a benevolent smile on Laura.

Who said, "I think I'm going to be too busy to—" She apparently saw the hurt on the children's faces because she stopped speaking abruptly. Her distraught gaze lifted to meet his. "Matt, do something!"

"Sure," he agreed. "How about we take the kids to the new Disney movie opening Friday?"

"Matt!" She stood up, glaring at him.

Jessica, however, was appeased. "That's a good beginning," she said, "if you just remember to hug and kiss a lot." She waved a grubby hand. "'Bye-bye, Zach. See you Friday."

"'Bye-bye." He waved back, then looked up at his mother. "So when we getting married to Jessica's daddy?"

Matt didn't wait for the answer to that one. Grabbing Jessica's sticky hand, he hauled her toward the door. Abby leaped aside and he made his getaway, well aware that it was for the moment only.

They hadn't broken it gently to the children at all and now they were in deeper than ever.

When Laura went into work the next day, April Forbes said a muffled "Hello" and looked quickly away. Was that a smile trying to break loose on the receptionist's face? And what did *she* have to be smiling about? Laura wondered crossly.

Laura figured she had plenty of trouble without worrying about April's hidden motives. Like Matt, for example. What was wrong with her, letting him get so close to breaching her defenses?

If they ever ran out of people willing to interrupt them, no telling *what* would happen.

She tossed her purse into the bottom drawer of her desk and clicked on the computer. Before she could pick up her dummy sheets, Katy entered the newsroom and crossed to stand before Laura's desk.

"So how's it going?" she asked with a crafty smile.

"Fine," Laura said shortly, turning back to her work and hoping Katy would take the hint.

Being Katy, she wouldn't know a hint if it kicked her in the shin. "I hear you had a real nice time last night," she said, sitting down in the interviewee chair.

Laura gave her friend a sharp glance. "Who told you that?"

Katy shrugged. "I forget. Matt dropped by, did he?"

"You were there when he asked if he could." Laura tapped impatiently at the computer keys to pull up the story she'd been editing just before going home yesterday. It hadn't been right but she'd been in no mood to figure out what it needed.

Like she was now.

Katy didn't say anything else but she didn't leave, either. After a minute to two, Laura looked up with a frown. Katy looked exactly like a Cheshire cat disguised as a woman.

She leaned forward eagerly. "So tell me everything!"

"About *what?*"

"About you and Matt, what else?"

"Katy Andrews, how many times do I have to tell you? There *is* no me and Matt."

"Oh, no? Then why were the two of you making out in your kitchen?"

Laura gasped. "Who told you that?"

"Roger Reedy over at city hall."

"Roger!" My God, this was awful. "Where did *he* hear it?"

"You want chapter and verse? Okay, as I recall—"

Katy ticked off names on her fingers. "Roger heard it from the mayor, who heard it from her daughter, who heard it from her son who's a teenage kid who occasionally dates Abby Royce, your baby-sitter." She looked very pleased with herself. "Did I miss anyone?"

"I doubt it." Laura's shoulders slumped. "The whole town's talking about us again, I take it."

"I'd say that's a fair assessment of the situation. So what happened? Did he put any serious moves on you or did he—"

"Katy, stop cross-examining me." Laura jumped out of her chair. "You'll have to excuse me now. I need to talk to the people in composing."

"Spoilsport!" Katy called after her friend. "What's wrong with a little healthy interest in a friend?"

Laura could think of many, many answers to that question.

Matt endured the Day From Hell for as long as he could and then stomped into his grandfather's office in high dudgeon. Careful not to slam the door behind him, he stalked to the desk, planted his fists and leaned over to glare into John's bemused eyes.

"You've ruined my life!" he roared.

"How so?" John waved his outraged grandson into a chair.

"By running that Prince Charming ad in the newspaper, that's how." Matt slumped into the chair. "I can't get anything done in this town because everybody's too interested in my love life—ha!—to let me.''

"So how *is* your love life?" John inquired.

"Nonexistent!"

"That's not what *I* hear."

Matt felt wounded to the quick. "Et tu, Grandpa?" he inquired gloomily.

John laughed. "Perk up, my boy! All those people making a fuss—they're just jealous. Laura is a lovely lady and—"

"Not available."

"Of course, she's available. She's a widow."

Matt shook his head. "That doesn't make her available. She isn't interested in me, period."

"But you're interested in her," John guessed shrewdly.

Matt's usually quick tongue failed him. After a moment, he sighed and said seriously, "I might be, under other circumstances. We're just not interested in the same things, Grandpa. For openers, she's a perfectionist and I'm a slob."

"You're not a slob, Matt, you're a man. Women are supposed to be perfectionists. Otherwise, nobody would be able to walk across the living room floor without tripping. It's God's way."

Matt laughed despite himself. "Grandpa, it's a good thing the Political Correctness faction didn't hear that."

"Wouldn't matter," John said. "Us old guys can get away with telling the truth while you young folks get all stirred up trying to find ways of saying what you mean without saying what you mean."

"I think there may be a kernel of truth in there somewhere but I'm not sure where." Matt sighed. "I've gotta get away for a few days," he announced suddenly. "Just me and Jessica—someplace where I can do some serious thinking."

"About...?"

"Me. My life. Jessica and what's best for her." He grinned wryly. "World peace. The Universe. The Cosmos. Why is there air?"

John smiled. "I'd say for all that, what you need is peace and quiet. Want to use the cabin?"

Good old grandpa. "Yes. Is it available?"

"For you, I'd evict. Of course it's available. When do you want it?"

"Next week? I'd like to go up Monday."

"You got it." John opened a desk drawer, fished around inside and came up with a set of keys. "Everything should be there and be working. Just take your own food and clean up when you leave."

"Thanks, Grandpa." Matt meant it with all his heart.

"You're welcome." John's expression grew serious. "I hope you find the answers you're looking for, Matt. Just remember, every human being wants the same thing. We just look for it in different ways."

Matt stood up. "You can't leave it there," he said, fighting sarcasm. "What *is* this universal thing we're all after? Money? Power? Fame? Sex?"

"I'm not about to fall for your nonsense," John said quietly. "It's love, and you darned well know it."

* * *

Laura called the mayor later in the morning with an ulterior motive. "Any chance you could do lunch today?" she inquired.

"Hmmm." Marilyn managed to convey volumes with that inarticulate sound. "For you—sure. But I need to make it later...say one at the Rawhide Café?"

"That will be fine—and thank you."

Gratified, Laura hung up the phone. What she had to say she could say to John, but her boss was Matt's grandfather and she'd just as soon not get him involved if she could help it....

"So," Mayor Marilyn said, pouring sugar into her iced tea, "to what do I owe this honor?"

Laura smiled. "I'm the one who's honored. Lunch with the mayor!"

"And I'm lunching with the life-styles editor of the Rawhide *Review!*" Marilyn lifted her glass in a salute. "Here's to us, two powerful women buttering each other up like crazy!"

Laura laughed and clinked glasses. "*Are* you buttering me up?"

"Sure am," Marilyn admitted. "I'd like to get a little extra publicity for the forty-fifth annual Rawhide City Ice Cream Social. We'll have several out-of-town bigwigs there, including our state senator, so I'd like to have a decent turnout."

"No problem," Laura agreed readily. "Glad to help."

"I knew you would be." Marilyn cocked her head. "Now it's your turn. What can I do for you, Laura?"

She licked her lips. "I wonder...could I use your

cabin for a few days next week? If no one else has
spoken first, of course.''

"You've got it. Come back to the office with me
after lunch and I'll give you the keys and directions.
You've never been there, have you?''

Laura shook her head.

"Then I'll draw you a map," Marilyn promised.
"It's not hard to find if you know where you're going.
It is quite isolated, though.''

"That's what I want," Laura said. "Solitude…just
Zach and me and a chance to do some serious thinking.''

"About Matt," Marilyn said.

Laura's head jerked up. "You, too?''

Marilyn smiled gently. "Honey, I know there's
never been anything between you and Matt, and I
know you've been thrown together to keep Jessica
from being hurt. But you're both such special people
that I have to wonder if proximity might reveal a
person different from what you expected.''

"So far, that hasn't happened," Laura said stiffly.

"Maybe you're afraid to let it happen.''

Afraid? Laura didn't like to think she was afraid of
anything. She didn't dare to be, when she had sole
responsibility for the safety and welfare of a precious
young life. But as she and the mayor ate and talked
and laughed together, the thought kept tugging at the
back of her mind: she *was* afraid, but not of Matt.

She, self-disciplined perfectionist Laura Gilliam,
was afraid of herself…and of what that scoundrel
Matt Reynolds did to her self-control.

*   *   *

"John?" Marilyn shifted the telephone to the other ear. "I just wanted to let you know I've given Laura the cabin next week.... You *what?*" She burst into laughter. "You're absolutely right," she said after listening for a moment. "Even Prince Charming and Cinderella need an occasional nudge. Let's pretend we never had this conversation." She hung up, still chuckling.

It took a lot of hugs and kisses and "pleases" to get Grandpa to take her downtown to buy a new dress, but Jessica finally managed it. "Daddy said he'd take me but he's busy building Mrs. Laura's new house again," she confided.

Grandpa rolled his eyes. "That job's *still* not finished?"

"Daddy says it would be but she keeps changing her mind. Daddy says—"

His laughter cut her off. "Jess, you're a real little magpie."

She loved learning new words, so she asked, "What's a madpie?"

"That's magpie, and it's a bird that never shuts up."

That tickled her fancy. "Then I guess I *am* like that bird," she agreed. She could use that on Zach, who talked more than she did. "Com' on, let's go in here." And grabbing his hand, she hauled him into the Zenith Department Store on Main Street.

They emerged fifteen minutes later, a big box tucked safely beneath Grandpa's arm. Inside was the most beautiful dress in the world: all pink and ruffled and laced and pearled. Jessica felt aglow just thinking about how gorgeous it was.

Boy, would Mrs. Laura be surprised when Jess wore it to the movies Friday night.

One of grandpa's friends called his name.

"Wait right here for me," Grandpa said, pointing to the sidewalk in front of the BonTon Bootery. He walked a few steps away to join his friend at the curb and was quickly involved in a noisy conversation.

Jessica didn't mind waiting. The big glass window at the Bootery was full of all kinds of boots and shoes. When I grow up, she promised herself, I'm going to wear shoes with great big high heels so I'll be taller than the boys. Or maybe I'll wear boots, so I can kick boys in the shins if they mess with me.

Boys were a real pain sometimes. Then a brand new thought occurred to her, that perhaps men were an equally big pain to women—but no, that wasn't likely. Look at her daddy, for example. He was the best daddy in the world and not a big pain at all. Who wouldn't love him? Her daddy was...she stopped thinking to stare.

She couldn't believe what she saw: the most beautiful shoes in the world. They were kind of off to one side, half-hidden by an ugly black pair, but she spotted them just the same.

Cinderella slippers.

She could see through them; were they really made of glass? And they had super-high heels, and a silver buckle across the front.

Oh, they were gorgeous! Mrs. Laura would look

beautiful in them. If Daddy gave her those shoes, she'd hug him and kiss him for sure.

But Daddy wouldn't buy shoes for a lady. Jessica knew that without even asking. Look at the way she had to nag him to get a new dress.

Maybe, just maybe, Jessica could buy the shoes herself and hide them in her closet in case of emergency. Like, if Mrs. Laura and Daddy had a fight, Jessica could pull out the magic shoes—any shoes that beautiful had to be magic—and they'd make up again.

Jessica licked her lips. How much did such beautiful, magical shoes cost? The big orange sign above them shouted Sale! so maybe they'd be really cheap. Holding her breath, she pressed her cheek against the window and strained to see the price tag. Ah, she finally had it—

She gulped. Twenty-seven dollars and ninety-five cents on *sale?*

And here she stood without a penny to her name. Daddy would give her an allowance Saturday, if she didn't screw up too bad before then, but five dollars sure wasn't enough to buy those shoes. She glanced at Grandpa, still talking to his friend, but she knew it wouldn't be right to ask him for the return of her piggy bank.

So where might she be able to get her hands on twenty-seven dollars and ninety-five cents?

"Hi, short stuff."

Jessica glanced around to find Aunt Katy standing there. "Hi back," she said.

"I haven't seen much of you lately," Katy said. "Are you having a good summer?"

Jessica shrugged. "It could be better."

Katy laughed. "I thought you'd be all excited because your ad is working so well."

"My ad?" Jessica frowned. "Oh, you mean Prince Charming."

"That's right." Katy frowned. "You don't look happy. I thought you liked Laura."

"I like her a lot!" Jessica was outraged to imagine anyone would think otherwise.

"Then what's the matter?"

Jessica's shoulders drooped. "It's not going so awful good," she admitted.

"Oh, dear." Katy looked genuinely sorry to hear this. "Do you know what the problem is?"

"Well…" Jessica looked around to make sure nobody was listening, especially her father or Zach's mother. "I think they're just doing it for the children."

Katy broke into laughter. "Doing it for the children?"

Jessica nodded firmly. "They keep trying to tell us they don't want to get married but Zach's too little and I pretend I don't get it. So they just keep on acting like they like each other. I keep thinking they'll catch on someday…duh! Like it takes a genius to know."

"To know what?" Katy asked, and she wasn't laughing.

"That we belong together," Jessica said, "me and

Zach and Daddy and Mrs. Laura. But I'm getting kind of worried...." She sighed.

So did Katy. "I think you all belong together, too," she said. "I wish there was something I could do."

"There is!" Jessica couldn't pass up a chance like this.

Katy looked startled. "Like what?"

Jessica licked her lips. "See those shoes?" She pointed.

Katy craned her neck, then winced. "Good lord, I've never seen anything so..."

Eagerly Jessica filled in the missing word. "Beautiful?"

"I was thinking of something *fairly* close to that." Katy frowned. "But I don't understand."

"Simple. Daddy is Prince Charming and Mrs. Laura is Cinderella, right? And how did the prince know who Cinderella was? He..." She urged the answer from Katy.

"...tried on the glass slipper and it fit?"

Jessica beamed. "Exactly! Only I don't think Daddy would buy shoes for Mrs. Laura, do you? I could buy them, though, and have 'em handy in case of emergency! I mean, if I just had twenty-seven dollars and ninety-five cents...."

"Plus tax," Katy added.

Jessica sighed. "I forgot about that." She looked at Aunt Katy out of the corner of her eye. "I don't suppose you...might like to loan me the money?"

"Do you have any collateral?"

"Maybe. What is it?"

"Do you own anything worth twenty-seven dollars

and ninety-five cents that I could have if you didn't pay me? That's collateral.''

This was sounding kind of serious but buying those shoes was too important to get scared. ''My dog, Fluffy, cost a hundred dollars when he was a puppy. Now that he's grown he's probably worth a whole lot more.''

''Hmmm. Let me think.''

Jessica watched anxiously, wishing she knew what Katy was thinking about. Sometimes grown-ups were hard to figure. It seemed so obvious to Jessica; those shoes could be the key to her future.

Katy straightened. ''Tell you what, if you can't come up with the money and you still think you need those shoes, check back with me later.''

Jessica felt a touch of desperation. ''But what if they're gone? What if someone else buys them first?''

''Somehow I doubt that will happen,'' Katy said reassuringly. ''Trust me on that.''

''But—''

''Jessica, darling, who do I look like, a fairy god-mother? Now do as I say, and if you really really want to buy those shoes and you can't come up with the money anywhere else, come see me again.''

Jessica watched her walk away, thinking that some-times grown-ups, even the nice ones, could be dumb as a rock without half trying.

CHAPTER EIGHT

MATT and Laura took the kids to Denver Saturday to see the latest Disney film. The youngsters were in high spirits; the adults weren't.

Matt had picked them up in his huge red pickup truck with the extended cab, which provided seating for the children. On the way down the mountain, she tried to maintain a cool, detached manner but be reasonably friendly at the same time. What had happened in her kitchen had made them awkward, Laura concluded, uncomfortably trying to make polite conversation.

The kiss had, in her opinion, been unseemly and must never be repeated. There was absolutely no possibility of any kind of long-term relationship with a Lothario like Matt Reynolds, and Laura was not the kind of woman who ran around kissing attractive men just because they were handy.

So why did she keep letting two pint-size cupids push her into corners she didn't want to be in?

Matt thought that Laura seemed even more aloof and cool than usual—which was considerable. He figured the kitchen clinch had led to this awkwardness, but he couldn't actually say he'd mind trying that again just on general principles.

He'd never run into a woman as elusive as the one

currently trying to make polite conversation as they rumbled down the mountainside. The kiss had really rattled her cage; she'd shut down her vulnerable side completely.

Although there was absolutely no possibility of any kind of long-term relationship with a woman this re-pressed and uncooperative, he was not the kind of man who could resist a challenge. He doubted he'd be able to rest until he'd figured out what made the luscious Laura—damn, that's what Dylan had called her—tick.

They rounded a curve and the city of Denver lay spread out on the plain below them. Matt, taking the onramp to the highway, reminded himself that he was simply a victim of circumstances—circumstances re-sulting from his daughter's decision to take matters into her own hands.

He might not be happy about the outcome but he supposed he'd just have to make the best of it....

The movie was...a Disney cartoon; what more was there to say? Laura tried to concentrate but again and again found her attention drawn to the man sitting on the aisle staring straight ahead. He seemed as totally engrossed as the children in the bright action on the screen.

Laura had maneuvered the children between the adults when they'd chosen their seats, figuring that if she ended up beside Matt it would be the longest two hours of her life. Even so, time dragged and when the houselights came on, she breathed a sigh of relief.

Zach was full of enthusiasm for the film. "Boy," he gushed, "I really liked the fighting part!"

"Me, too." Matt kept his seat, letting the mob of children and long-suffering adults stream up the aisle. "That was my favorite."

Jessica's tone was superior. "I liked the part in the garden, with all the pretty flowers and birds."

"Girls!" Zach looked to Matt for support, which was promptly forthcoming.

"We liked the guy stuff," Matt agreed, "not the chick stuff."

"Chick stuff?" Zach looked puzzled, then giggled. *"Chick stuff!"*

"Well," Laura said, her haughty tone matching Jessica's, "*I* liked the chick stuff, too."

They argued about "chick stuff versus guy stuff" all the way out to the parking lot. Once they were seated inside the big pickup, Matt turned toward Laura. "Want to stop and grab a bite to eat on the way home?" he asked.

"Oh, I don't think that's a good—"

"Please, Mama? *Please?*"

"Please, Mrs. Laura?"

Laura sighed. "Looks as if I'm outnumbered."

Matt grinned. "Not to mention outmaneuvered." He raised his voice. "So what'll it be, kids? Hamburgers, pizza—"

"A place that serves vegetables?" But Laura's was a voice crying in the wilderness and they ended up at PizzaRita's.

The remains of two pizzas lay before them on the wooden picnic table topped with a bright red-and-white-checked plastic tablecloth: one slice of "Rita's Meat Lovers Deluxe Special" smothered with every indigestible meat product ever known to grace a pizza; and half of a "Veggy Delight."

Zach eyed Rita's special. "Can I have one more piece?" he asked hopefully. "Please, Mama?"

Laura sighed. "Sure, why not? I figure the harm's already done. How about you, Jessica? One more slice of Veggy Delight?"

"Yes, please," Jessica said primly. "I need to eat lots now because this is probably the last pizza I'll have until after our vacation."

Laura laughed and extracted a huge pie-shaped wedge of pizza, sliding it onto the girl's plate. "I can't imagine many places you could go on vacation that wouldn't have a pizza restaurant."

"We're going to a cabin in the mountains," the girl said. "There are no people for a hundred miles around."

Laura's blood ran cold. Could Matt and Jessica be planning to use John's cabin the same week she and Zach were slated to spend there? Surely not!

"Hey," Zach said, "us, too!"

"You, too, what?" Jessica wanted to know, daintily picking up green peppers that had fallen onto her plate and scattering them artistically on her pizza.

"Us, too, going to a cabin."

Matt looked up from his plate with an alarmed expression. "Really? Are we all talking about the cabin John and Marilyn own?"

Laura's stomach dropped. "Let's discuss this

later,'' she said hastily, adding in an attempt to change the subject, ''Shall we ask for a box to carry the rest of the pizza home?''

''I think we'd better discuss it now.'' Matt frowned. ''I take it from that evasive answer that we're all going to the same cabin. The question is…when?''

''Next week!'' both children shouted in unison. Startled, they stared at each other and then great big smiles broke over their faces.

''We're going camping together!'' Jessica exclaimed. ''Hooray! We'll have so much fun!''

Zach tugged on Matt's sleeve. ''Can you teach me to fish? Mama doesn't like to fish. She thinks worms are yucky.''

Jessica grabbed Laura's hand. ''I can show you how to make s'mores! That's my favorite. You need chocolate and marshmallows and graham crackers—''

''Not so fast!'' Matt held up his hands for silence. ''I think we've got a little problem here.''

''Or a big problem,'' Laura agreed. ''When I spoke to Marilyn, she said the cabin would be empty next week.''

''And when I spoke to Grandpa, he said the same.'' Matt cocked his head and his lips curved up almost seductively. ''I don't know how they could screw up the schedule this way. It's a good thing we found this out before we…''

She knew ''before we'' what: before they all showed up in the middle of nowhere at the same time.

A week in the wilderness with Matt Reynolds? She shivered with a mixture of dread and...anticipation.

Jessica turned her excited face toward her father. "Can we all drive up together, Daddy? Oh, this will be such fun! Thank you for a wonderful surprise. Thank you, too, Mrs. Laura."

"Slow down, Jess." Matt seemed to be going to extraordinary lengths to avoid looking at Laura. "Somebody's made a mistake, honey. We can't all go to the cabin the same week."

She looked taken aback. "Why not?"

Matt and Laura stared at each other.

Laura took a stab at it. "For openers, there's not enough room. John said there were only two bedrooms and—"

"There's room." Jessica, who'd been looking a little worried, perked up. "There's the grown-ups' bedroom with a great big bed and the kid bedroom with a bunch of bunk beds and stuff."

Laura felt her cheeks grow warm. "But we have *two* grownups, so that's a problem."

Jessica thought that over. "It wouldn't be if you guys got married," she said helpfully.

"Failing that," her father said, "we *do* still have a problem."

"No, we don't." Jessica got that stubborn look on her face. "Mrs. Laura can have the grown-up room and you can sleep in the kid room with me 'n' Zach."

"That's out of the question," Laura blurted. "I only want to go up there for a little peace and quiet. How can I think if..." The look on Jessica's face brought her fumbling to a halt. "What is it, honey?"

"I thought you liked me," the girl said in a suddenly thin voice.

"I do like you, only—"

Zach began to cry. "You don't like Jessica, Mama? *I* like Jessica."

"Of course I do. It's just that I—" Laura cast a desperate glance at Matt.

Who did his best. "Stop it, kids. You don't know what you're talking about. We can't just pack up and go camping together." He glanced at Laura for support.

"Why not?" Jessica sniffled.

"Because—because I don't think Laura's the camping type. She probably doesn't know anything about wilderness living."

Laura, who hadn't spent four years as a Girl Scout for nothing, glared at him. "Let's not get personal," she suggested tartly.

Jessica looked alarmed. "If Mrs. Laura doesn't know about cabins, maybe we need to look out for her and Zach," she said. "We wouldn't want anything to happen to them."

Her argument obviously made a dent of Matt's resolve. "You've got a point there, kid. Laura—"

"Oh, for goodness' sake!" She crumpled up her paper napkin and dropped it on her paper plate. "I was a Girl Scout! I can take care of myself, and Zach, too."

"But have you ever been alone in the Rocky Mountains? This cabin really is quite isolated."

"No, but I'm sure we'll do just fine."

Jessica leaned forward eagerly. "Do you know what to do if you get lost?"

"I won't get lost."

"But if you do?"

Zach had been following the conversation, his head swinging right and left as he listened. "If I got lost, I'd run to the cabin!" he declared with little-boy bravado. "If I saw a bear, I'd punch him in the nose!"

Jessica's air turned superior. "That would be wrong, Zach," she lectured him. "If you saw a bear, you wouldn't punch him 'cause you'd be scared to death. And if you got lost, you shouldn't go running all over. You should hug a tree."

Zach reeled back on the bench and nearly fell off, saved only by his mother's quick reaction. "I don't hug trees," he objected.

Jessica nodded emphatically. "When you get lost, you should pick a tree and hug it until somebody comes to save you. Right, Daddy?"

"That's right. But you don't have to hug the tree all the time, you can just sit down next to your tree and wait."

"Wait until Daddy saves you," Jessica elaborated.

"Now, Jess, we can't—"

"We can, Daddy! Me 'n' Zach *want* to. If we don't go camping together I'll—I'll—!" Words failed her but tears didn't, and they were soon rolling down her cheeks.

Zach watched her, wide-eyed, and then he, too, began to cry. "I wanna go camping with Jessica and her daddy," he sobbed. "Please, Mama?"

"Please, Daddy?"

Matt and Laura stared helplessly at each other. After a moment, he said tentatively, "I suppose we could give it a try, Laura."

"Oh, Matt!" Her stomach clenched into a tight little knot of foreboding. "I really don't want to do this."

"Neither do I," he said, his face tight. "How is it we keep digging this hole deeper and deeper when all we want to do is walk in the other direction?"

She shrugged, overcome by the thought of day after day alone in a mountain cabin with the attractive and mercurial Matt Reynolds and his manipulating but adorable daughter.

"So shall we give it a try? What harm can there be in it, really? We're adults...."

It would be easier if we were children, she thought—until she looked at the misery mixed with hope on the children's faces. "Maybe..."

Jessica leaped to the desired conclusion. "We're gonna go *camping!*" She scrambled off the bench. "Oh, Mrs. Laura, thank you! *Thank you!*" The little girl threw her arms around Laura's neck.

Over the slender shoulders, Laura's gaze met Matt's. She'd been about to say, "Maybe we could find something else to do together instead," but that was a moot response now. She couldn't possibly disappoint the two kids capering around the table and singing, "We're gonna go camping!" over and over again.

Heaven help her, she was committed.

Or maybe she should *be* committed.

* * *

A subdued Matt dropped off his passengers in a strained silence at Laura's house. "I'll give you a call about the cabin," he said.

She nodded without smiling. "We do need to talk about arrangements."

Back at his own house, he sent Jessica up to shower and get ready for bed while he opened a beer and wandered into the family room. He'd no more than settled down in his favorite chair when a knock on the door brought him swinging around.

Dylan stood there, looking uncharacteristically subdued. "Gotta minute?" he inquired.

"Sure." Matt stepped aside. "Come on in, buddy." Handing Dylan his untouched beer, he walked into the kitchen to grab another one for himself, then returned to the family room. "So what's up?"

"I just wanted to find out if you'd heard anything about Carl Stevens's accident...."

For a few moments they talked about the romantic problems that had landed a mutual friend in the hospital, the result of a bad case of unrequited love.

"I don't know if I oughta give him sympathy or kick his butt," Dylan finished in a disgusted tone. "How a guy can get so hung up on a woman that he loses all his common sense is more than I can understand."

Matt, who wasn't feeling all that wise himself at the moment, shrugged. "You were in love once. At least, you said you were when you married the woman."

"Yeah, and I learned my lesson in a hurry." Dylan

looked disgruntled. "When she packed up and walked, you didn't see me running around town wringing my hands and running my pickup truck into trees."

"Maybe not," Matt admitted, "but you had a couple of hard-drinking years there, right after she left."

Dylan flashed a pained grin. "I was extra thirsty there for a while. That's all over and done with now."

"Yeah, sure."

Dylan peered at his friend through narrowed eyes. "So how'd the date go today?" he asked abruptly.

"Date? It wasn't a *date,* exactly. We took the kids to a movie."

"That's all?"

"Then we took the kids for pizza."

"That's all?"

"Then we agreed we'd spend next week together at Grandpa's cabin in the mountains—want another beer?"

"Hell, no!" Dylan stared. "You...Laura Gilliam...alone together—"

"With two kids!"

"In an isolated mountain cabin? I don't think the kids are going to be enough protection." Dylan slumped back in his chair, his chin on his chest. "This time the luscious Laura's gonna tumble. This is getting downright depressing." Dylan, the kidder, was no longer kidding.

"No way," Matt protested, feeling disloyal to Laura for having to say it...not to mention like a liar for denying what had never completely left his mind from the day he saw her for the first time three years ago. He'd wanted her then; he wanted her now. But he didn't intend to take her. It would be much too...complicated. "Wanna tell me why you're so down in the mouth tonight?"

"Do I look like I've lost my best friend?" Dylan's smile wasn't all that convincing. "As a matter of fact, that's how it feels."

"After all we've been through together? Not a chance."

"Yeah, that's what you say but this romance is coming to a head in a real big hurry. Hell, it wouldn't surprise me if you came back an engaged man. In fact—I expect it."

Matt stared. "You're out of your cotton pickin' mind!"

Dylan shrugged. "I hate to sound like a bad sport but I've seen it before. Once you get her where you want her—"

"Put a cork in it," Matt growled. "This is not some big setup for a seduction or anything."

"It might as well be. You're not made of steel, my man. You'll wind up in bed before you come back down that mountain, whether you intend to or not. You know what they say about the best laid plans, et cetera."

"She's not that kind of woman," Matt protested— weakly, he feared.

"Don't be so sure. I've seen how she looks at you—hey, I've seen how you look at her. Once you sleep with her—"

"Dammit, Dylan, stop saying that." Matt sprang

to his feet and began to pace. "We're doing this for the kids. We're not gonna—"

"I'll bet dollars to donuts you will," Dylan cut off the protests. "Hell, I'll bet my genuine autographed Babe Ruth baseball that you and the luscious Laura come back down that mountain a couple—in the Biblical sense, I mean."

Matt choked on his beer. "Jeez, Dylan, I've been trying to weasel that baseball away from you ever since your dad gave it to you twenty-odd years ago."

"Twenty-one, which should prove how confident I am. If you're so damned sure, put up your genuine Stetson hat autographed by Slim Sloan. I've always wanted the autograph of the greatest bull rider the world has ever known."

"Wouldn't it be simpler just to trade?" Matt suggested.

"No," Dylan countered. "I want 'em both and this is an easy way to get 'em. Man, you are *hooked* and you don't even know it."

Matt strove for a self-assured sneer. "You're nuts. All I'd have to do is lie to you, say I didn't sleep with her even if I did."

Dylan didn't smile. "But you won't do that," he said. "You wouldn't lie to your best bud, even if there was nothing else at stake."

That, unfortunately, was probably true. Matt hesitated for a moment, then began, "Dylan, if you think I'm gonna—"

"Uncle Dylan!" Jessica flew into the room, arms outstretched. She wore pink pajamas, and wet hair streamed down her back. Hopping onto his lap, she kissed his cheek.

Over her shoulder, his eyes met those of his best friend. "Deal?"

Hell, Matt thought, there's no way Laura's gonna fall into my arms. "Deal!"

Matt called Laura early Sunday morning. "Just want to be sure we know what we're doing when we head up the mountain tomorrow," he said.

"Yes, of course." She felt completely removed from this conversation. Polite but distant, that was the ticket.

"The cabin's nice but it's still a cabin in the middle of nowhere," he said. "We don't need to take sheets or towels or any of that, but we need our personal stuff and enough food to last the course, since the nearest store is about twenty-five miles away."

"All right."

"Be practical, Laura." He sounded impatient. "Don't drag a lot of stuff up there that'll just be in the way."

"Thank you for sharing that," she said sarcastically, on the spot revising her "to take" list. "I know what I'm doing, Matt."

There was a long silence. Then he said, "I sure as hell hope one of us does."

"There's still time to call this off," she flared.

"Yeah, but if we do, you're the one who has to tell the kids."

That stopped her. "All right," she agreed reluctantly, "a-camping we will go."

"I'll pick you and Zach up Monday at six."

"A.M?"

"I like to get an early start."

"And I like to get a leisurely start."

"Split the difference—six-thirty."

"Forget it!" Struck by suspicion, she added, "And what do you mean, you'll pick us up?"

"Just what it sounds like."

"Forget that, too. I'm driving." No way did she want to be stuck on a mountaintop at his mercy.

The deep, annoyed intake of breath traveled clearly across the wire, but all he said was, "Fine. Suit yourself. In that case, you should follow me up in your own car. I'll still be there Monday at six-thirty."

"I'll be ready." She wouldn't be happy but she *would* be ready.

Laura looked absolutely adorable in close-fitting jeans, heavy hiking boots and a red plaid shirt that emphasized the thrust of her breasts and the trimness of her waist. She'd placed a floppy denim hat on top of her blond hair and, as far as Matt could tell, she wasn't wearing any makeup at all. That glow, he concluded was natural.

"Hi, Mr. Reynolds!" Zach came flying out the door to meet them. "I'm ready!"

"I see that." Matt smiled at the small boy in his jeans and boots and sweatshirt. He looked up at Laura, approaching more sedately. "Got anything I can throw in the back of the truck?"

"No, thanks. I'm already loaded and Lucy is at the neighbor's."

''Fluffy's with Uncle Dylan,'' Jessica offered. ''I wanted to take her but daddy said no, dogs always chase all the wildlife away.''

Laura smiled sympathetically. ''Uncle Dylan will take good care of her, I'm sure.'' She gestured toward her Jeep Cherokee. ''Zach and I are all ready to go.''

''I wanna ride with Jessica!'' Zach declared. ''Please, Mama?''

''Please?'' Jessica chimed in. ''Can Zach ride with me?''

Thus it happened that Matt drove up the mountain with the two kids in the back seat and Laura following in her red sport utility vehicle. He understood why she'd insisted upon driving herself and couldn't blame her.

She didn't want to be at his mercy.

And she didn't know the half of it. Damn that Dylan for planting all those thoughts in a mind that needed no such encouragement.

In the clearing before the log cabin, Laura leaped from the Jeep, too excited to linger. ''What a wonderful drive,'' she exclaimed. ''Matt, the scenery is gorgeous!''

''Sure is.'' He held the door for the kids. ''Don't you guys run off, now. You've got to help carry stuff inside.''

''Aw, Daddy!'' But it was only lip service, for Jessica was grinning ear to ear.

It took many trips but eventually everything that belonged inside was. While Matt instructed the two children in outdoor etiquette and safety, Laura explored her home-away-from-home for the next week.

As promised, it contained two bedrooms. The one on the right opened onto a fairly large room with king-size bed, a chest of drawers, two bedside tables and a small arrangement of table and two chairs. All were hewn from heavy logs that perfectly matched the cabin itself. A small bathroom completed the "master suite," if thus it could be called.

Laura pulled aside the cheerful yellow curtain at one window and peeked out. The forest came almost up to the house itself. Squirrels flashed across the frame provided by the window, and birds fluttered in and out of sight.

Beautiful. Peaceful. Inviting.

The second bedroom, on the left side of the combination kitchen-dining-family room and next to the other bathroom, was smaller and more crowded, with two sets of bunk beds and a single chest of drawers. Actually, its Spartan simplicity reminded Laura of a college dorm. None of the bedspreads matched but all were bright primary colors, as were the curtains on the two windows.

"I want a top bunk!" Jessica burst into the room and threw herself at the nearest ladder.

"I want a top bunk, too!" Zach was right behind her, launching himself at the other set of bunk beds.

"Zach, you've never slept on a top bunk before," Laura protested, moving to intercept him. "Don't you think—"

"Let him go, Laura."

Matt's hand on her arm stopped her even if his words didn't. She gave him a questioning glance.

"It's a guy thing," he said, his lips twisting in a wry grin.

"But he's just a *little* guy," she argued, feeling a flutter of unease. "What if he falls off?"

"If he does—which I'm sure he won't, but if he does—we'll pick him up and put him back into bed. Let him try, Laura."

Laura hesitated. Others had told her she tended to be too protective of Zach, but without a father around to share the responsibility—

Abruptly she turned and walked out into the great room. Being a single parent was not an easy road to walk. She spent a great deal of time wondering if she were being too strict or too lenient, too overprotective or too permissive. Tired of that endless debate with herself, she reached for the first of the many cardboard boxes she'd packed. The first thing she pulled out was a lace tablecloth.

His sharp intake of breath startled her.

"What the hell is that?"

"A tablecloth," she said, suddenly glad she'd packed it. Holding it by one edge, she wafted it over the heavy wood-carved table and let it drift into place. She set an empty crystal vase in the middle and stood back to admire the effect.

"You're amazing," he said, and he didn't sound critical at all—simply amazed. "When I saw how you were dressed, I thought—" He shrugged, and his grin was charming. "I can't wait to see what else you've brought."

The kids skipped into the room. "Can we go outside, Daddy?" Jessica inquired.

"Do both of you remember the rules?"

Twin nods were vehement.

"We'll stay right in the front yard," Zach promised.

"Then you can go, but don't screw up." Matt gave them a mock ferocious glare. "Stay in the clearing right in front, and leave the door open so we can keep an eye on you." As they rushed for the exit, he added, "And don't mess around in the ashes inside that fire ring! Got it?"

"Got it!"

He laughed softly and Laura began to relax the tiniest little bit. He truly could be charming when he chose.

He turned to her, still smiling. "So what did you bring to eat?"

"Bananas, salad, trail mix, bread, eggs, baking mix, canned tuna and chili, caviar—"

"Caviar?" He stared at her incredulously. "You brought caviar to a mountain cabin?"

"I wanted to bring champagne but I was afraid it would give you ideas."

His expression was priceless. She turned aside to hide the smile tugging at her lips. "Okay, I confess— no caviar. I'm putting you on."

His laughter warmed her. "You're too much," he said. "Just about the time I think I have you figured out—"

"Give it up," she ordered airily. "Figuring me out isn't worth the effort. I haven't even managed to do that myself.'' She hadn't, either. One minute she wanted to run and hide while the next, she wanted to flirt with him. What had her mother told her about playing with fire? Even big girls could get burned... ''So what *did* you bring to eat?'' she asked breathlessly.

''Cans of beans, lots of hot dogs and marshmallows, plenty of cookies and candy bars and potato chips.'' He pounded his fists on his chest. ''Man food.''

''Junk food.'' She pursed her lips and shook her head in censure. ''It's a wonder you and that poor little girl don't have beriberi or some other dread disease by now, the way you eat.'' As she spoke, she began to empty the boxes of food, placing the contents on open shelves near the stainless steel sink.

After a moment, he did likewise with his supplies. ''Just like a woman,'' he grumbled, ''expecting a man to live on rabbit food. I'll bet your husband was a skinny little guy—''

They both stopped short, aware that he'd somehow crossed the line.

''I'm sorry,'' he began. ''I didn't mean any disrespect toward your husband but—''

A scream rent the air and they both froze.

Jessica was in trouble.

CHAPTER NINE

"WHERE—what—who—!"

Matt hit the center of the clearing at a dead run, Laura at his heels. Jessica stood next to the fire ring, eyes closed and fists clenched at her sides, screaming at the top of her lungs. Zach stood beside her with his eyes round as buttons and his expression frightened.

Laura grabbed her son and Matt grabbed his daughter. He gave her a shake. "What is it, Jess? What's the matter?"

"I saw a bear!" She pointed with a trembling forefinger. "You saw it, too, right, Zach?"

"Uhhh…" Zach glanced around with frightened eyes. "No."

"You did so! It was right there!" She began to cry.

"There, there." Matt patted her shoulder but his attention was on the pine trees circling this small clearing deep in the middle of the Rocky Mountains. "Wait here and let me take a look."

Jess sniffled. "Okay, Daddy."

"Do you think you should?" Laura asked anxiously. "If there's a bear out there—"

"Don't worry." He headed for the trees, pleased by her concern. Made him feel all manly.

When he returned, she'd taken the children inside

and calmed them down. Jessica, in fact, looked sheep-ish.

Laura glanced up from the pitcher of lemonade she'd been stirring. "Find anything?"

"I'm not sure. Jessica—?"

She hung her head but said nothing.

"Were you trying to scare Zach?"

"Well…maybe a little," she admitted, swallowing hard.

"And you ended up scaring yourself, is that right?"

Zach leaped to his feet from his seat at the wooden table. His eyes were wild. "She said a bear would come carry me off if I didn't do everything she told me. She said—"

"Okay, okay, we get the picture." Matt patted the boy's shoulder. "She's not going to pull *that* again. Right, Jessica?"

She shook her head without enthusiasm. "I'm sorry, Zach."

"You should be," Matt said, "because I did find bear sign out there."

Laura gasped. "You're kidding!"

"Nope. It was old but it was there. So let this be a lesson to all of you. No more fooling around and trying to scare each other. And everyone must do exactly as I say, for the safety of all of us. Is that agreed? Because if it's not, we can load all this stuff back up and go home."

A long silence greeted this option. Then Zach said in a small voice, "I don't wanna go home."

"Then you'll follow the rules?"

He shook his head with determination.

"I agree, Daddy," said the second little voice.

"Me, too," agreed the third voice—not quite so little. Laura smiled at them all. "I'm sure we all wish this hadn't happened but we've learned a valuable lesson. Let's forget about it and talk about our plans for the rest of the day. What does everyone want to do?"

"Go fishin'!" Zach shouted.

"Pick wildflowers and look at the animals!" Jessica shouted.

Matt looked at Laura. "There's a stream running alongside a meadow not far from here. Zach and I can fish and you and Jessica can explore, if that's okay."

"I'd like that."

"Then—let's go!"

They returned hours later, tired but happy. They brought with them a handful of wildflowers and weeds, already wilting in Jessica's warm grip, but not a single fish.

"We'll have better luck tomorrow," Matt promised the disappointed boy. "Remember, fishing calls for patience."

Laura wasn't sure Zach knew what "patience" was but he nodded and tried to be brave about it. "Why don't you put our bouquet in a glass of water and I'll start supper," she suggested.

"So what's on your menu?" Matt asked, looking interested.

"Chicken and noodles." She gave him an oblique glance.

"Yum!" Jessica set the glass of greenery on the table. "That sounds good."

"What's on *your* menu?" Laura inquired.

"Hot dogs."

"I love hot dogs!" Zach looked anxious. "Do I hav'ta eat noodles, Mama?"

"Do I hav'ta eat hot dogs?" Jessica looked equally anxious.

Matt looked at Laura with a big grin on his face. "Wanna trade kids for supper? You females can get all fancy-dancy while us men get all *manly*. We'll eat with our hands and use our jeans for napkins, stuff like that."

Laura couldn't help laughing. "I don't mind trading kids but I veto the use of jeans for napkins."

"Okay, we'll compromise."

"Hooray!" Zach jumped up and down. "Can I help cook, Mr. Reynolds?"

"I'm counting on it, partner. Com' on, I'll teach you how to build a safe campfire."

Laura watched the tall man usher the small boy out of the cabin and something tightened in the back of her throat. Matt was giving Zach something he'd never had before...a role model very like a father.

The hot dogs were good—well, as good as hot dogs got. But Matt couldn't help noticing the enticing aromas wafting from the open cabin door. It wasn't chicken, either; it was cinnamon he smelled. If chocolate turned him off, cinnamon in any form turned him on. By the time he finished the last of his four hot dogs, his mouth was watering.

Zach finished his second hot dog and, sure enough, wiped his fingers on his jeans. Matt was glad Laura wasn't around to see it.

"Yum," the little boy said. "Can we have Mama's Apple Surprise for dessert?"

Mama's Apple Surprise. Hmmm... Matt said innocently, "Do you think she'll give us any? I've got some candy bars—"

"Apple Surprise is better," Zach said seriously.

"Well," Matt said with feigned indifference, "if you want to go ask her, it's all right with me."

He stayed by the embers of their campfire while Zach ran inside. The murmur of voices, and then Laura calling, "Come on in if you'd like to join us for dessert, Matt."

Ah, he thought, rising from his log seat, this is living. Off into the wilderness with good food, good kids...and a good woman. Maybe Dylan was right and something *would* come of it.

Cabin cleaned and kids tucked into bed, Laura had no further reason to procrastinate. Taking a deep breath, she joined Matt on the log beside the small campfire. Flames leaped and crackled inside a fire ring of flat rocks.

When she approached, he looked up with an absent smile. He held a long stick with which he periodically poked at the fire. She found herself wishing *she* had a stick for poking, too. It would give her something to do to take her mind off the compelling presence of the man at her side.

He smiled at her over his shoulder, the fire and the moonlight casting intriguing shadows over the strong contours of his face. ''I'd say our first day went pretty well.''

''Yes.'' She licked her lips. ''You've very good with Zach. I want you to know how much I appreciate it. I know he needs a man's attention but...'' She shrugged.

''That's not all he needs. He also needs a father. You ever thought about getting married again?''

The question was impertinent but asked with such quiet seriousness that she couldn't take offense. ''Of course I've thought about it, but it's easier said than done.'' She darted him a defensive glance. ''I expect you know that, though.''

He sighed. ''Yeah, I do. Jessica never lets me forget it. She's always trying to set me up with some woman or other. This Prince Charming thing is the most off-the-wall thing she's done so far, though.''

''I guess she's desperate.''

''Yeah. She doesn't understand that there's more to finding a wife than asking for volunteers who are pretty and who like kids and pets.'' He looked into the depths of the fire, as if he could find answers there. ''I mean, you're pretty and like kids and pets, just for example.''

''I'm pretty?'' Hearing him say so warmed her.

''You know you're pretty.'' He gave her an incredulous glance. ''But you've never warmed to me, so in spite of the efforts of a couple of determined kids—''

''I've never *warmed* to you?'' She bit her lip to keep from laughing. She'd warmed to him *too* much, right from the beginning. But then he'd proven to be just as shallow as all the other men she'd met or dated after her husband's death. One lousy dinner, one lousy movie and they thought they had the right to start grabbing.

He scowled. ''What's so funny?''

''Nothing.''

''I don't believe you.''

''Suit yourself.'' She rose abruptly and stood looking down at him. ''I think I'll go inside now.''

''Don't.'' His voice had become low, intimate. ''Somehow I think we're starting to close in on whatever it was that put us so at odds with each other.''

''I have no idea what you're talking about.'' She started to turn away.

He caught her wrist in a light grip which she could easily have broken but didn't. ''Laura, don't go. Sit back down and talk to me.''

''Boy,'' she said incredulously, ''this is a switch— a guy wanting to talk!''

''Yeah, and don't think I like it.'' He released her arm and began poking at the fire again with his stick. ''It's just that I can't figure you out, even after knowing you for three years.''

She sat back down beside him. ''Can I have your stick?'' She reached for it.

''You want my stick?'' He pulled it beyond her reach.

"Please?"

"Well, hell." He handed it over and added, "Why did you slap my face the first time I tried to kiss you?"

"Because I knew that was the only reason you took me out—you and every other guy I dated after my husband died. 'Com' on, you're a widow, you have needs—!'" She poked viciously at the fire, sending sparks crackling toward the dark sky. "I hated all that grabbing, if you want to know the truth."

"So *that* was it." He sucked in a deep breath. "I almost went nuts trying to figure out why you slugged me. I mean, I didn't try to carry you off to bed or anything."

"No, but you would have," she shot back, feeling reckless.

"Yeah, maybe, but all you had to say was 'no.' You didn't have to slug me." He stared at her, his eyes narrowed to dark slits. "Did you run into someone who wouldn't take 'no' for an answer?"

She hadn't talked about this to anyone but found herself spilling it now. "He took 'no' for an answer, all right, but it required considerable convincing." As in a blouse ripped nearly off and bruise marks on her wrists, but at least she'd had the pleasure of seeing a quick karate toss leave him flat on his back and gasping for air.

"Want me to break his legs?" Matt asked, and he sounded serious.

That made her laugh, and it was as if in so doing she cast off the last shreds of trauma caused by that long-ago encounter. "Actually, I took care of him myself, once I realized what was going on. I studied karate as a kid and I finally got to use it.''

"I'm impressed. But jeez, Laura, surely you didn't think I was the kind of guy who'd—''

"I *didn't* think,'' she said quickly, "I reacted.'' She faced him straight-on. "I'm sorry now, but it was too fresh in my mind at the time.''

"Do you still feel the same way?''

She licked her lips. "The same way…?''

He gave her a slow, sexy smile. "I've got a hankering to know what I've been missing with you. It's against my better judgment but…I never intended…but you've got a way about you, Laura, that I find well-nigh irresistible.'' He straddled the log and put his hands lightly on her shoulders. "If I kissed you now, would you karate chop me into submission?''

"Why don't you try it and find out.'' She couldn't believe she'd said that!

"I think I'll just do that.''

Holding her lightly by the shoulders, he leaned closer while drawing her toward him at the same time, until their lips met. Laura closed her eyes, wondering at the feeling of recklessness that engulfed her. Everything was changing around her—her world, her feelings, her defenses.

He deepened the kiss and she sighed and slid her arms beneath his, around his waist. He felt so solid and real, so masculine and in control. Nothing bad could happen to her while he held her, because he *wasn't* the kind of man who'd try to take advantage of her. She hadn't been ready to see that, before.

Now she was.

He lifted his head. She opened her eyes and they stared at each other. She wondered if he felt the same amazement that sparked through her bloodstream.

He touched her trembling lips with his thumb. "I don't want to stop," he said in a husky voice.

"But you will—*we* will," she said, pulling on every last ounce of self-control to sit up straight, away from him. "I'm…a little embarrassed that I revealed so much to you."

"Don't be," he said quickly. "I needed to know."

"But you haven't shared anything about your own marriage."

He shrugged. "It wasn't as happy as yours. We were both too young. If she'd lived…well, not too many people with her type of leukemia do, but if she had, I don't think the marriage would have lasted." He sighed. "It was worth all the grief, though, because she gave me Jessica."

"Jessica is a great kid."

"Yeah, I think so. Zach is, too."

She laughed breathlessly. "We seem to have a mutual admiration society going on here, at least as far as our kids are concerned."

"It might even go past that. Laura—" He didn't touch her again, just nailed her with the power of his gaze. "Let's give this a chance between us, okay? We'll be here for six more days. Before we go back to civilization, I want to know if this crazy feeling I have for you is something that's going to last or—"

"Or," she agreed softly. "You're right, it is a crazy feeling and we do need to know what it means.'' This time she made it all the way to her feet. ''I've got to sleep on this, Matt. Good night.''

''Good night, Laura.''

As she walked away, she heard him murmur, ''At least she didn't karate chop me into little pieces.'' She entered the cabin smiling.

And trembling…

The kiss changed everything.

Laura no longer felt as if she had to hold anything back; she could let him see the pleasure she took in just having him near her, in the antics of the children, in the splendid isolation of what was turning into a dream vacation. She'd come here to think but all she thought about was him: Matt's kiss, his embrace, his humor and his honesty.

Could she be falling in love with a man she'd known and more or less detested for at least three years?

''Look, Mama! I caught this giant fish!''

Laura patted her smiling son on his tousled head. ''It's a beautiful fish,'' she praised him, carefully keeping her attention on the child instead of the man beaming at them both.

''Daddy—'' Zach broke off; he was making that mistake more and more often and it confused and embarrassed him. ''*Jessica*'s daddy showed me how to put the worm on all by myself,'' he said, righting his mistake.

But *was* it all that much of a mistake? Laura's gaze met Matt's and she knew he wondered the same thing.

* * *

From day one, it was "boys versus the girls," as Jessica put it; or "guy stuff" and "chick stuff," according to Zach. The little boy just naturally gravitated to Matt and Jessica to Laura.

Of course, some things they did together: tramped through the forest on picnics, swam in the hot springs, learned from Matt the difference between a rabbit track and a fox track.

And once in a while, Laura would see her son looking at Matt with adoration in his eyes—the same adoration she saw in Jessica's eyes—and she'd have to steady herself with a little pep talk.

Matt was interested in something besides sex; she knew he was. He wasn't setting her up by pretending an interest in her son.

He wouldn't *do* that to her.

And so the days passed…

"Look what I did, Daddy!" Jessica set a glass of wildflowers on the table with a flourish. "Mrs. Laura taught me how to arrange flowers. Like, see how the short ones are in the front and the tall ones in the back? Then I filled in all the holes with leaves and stuff."

Matt looked impressed. "You did that yourself?"

Jessica's grin stretched wider. "Not only that, when we get home Mrs. Laura will teach me how to sew on buttons so I can take care of you, and she's going to teach me how to bake brownies. Then maybe she'll teach me how to do the laundry, because you're always fading stuff all over my sheets—"

The little girl rattled on while Matt just sat there

with an attentive smile on his face. But slowly his gaze lifted until it met Laura's and what she read there made her catch her breath.

Matt and Zach opened their jar of peanut butter and used a table knife to spread it rather messily on slices of bread. The looks they gave Laura and Jessica were superior indeed.

Laura grinned at the girl. "Shall we show them how to make a peanut butter sandwich?" she asked.

"Let's!"

Jessica scooped peanut butter into a mixing bowl while Laura pulled a bag of shredded carrots from the cooler, then took bags of sunflower seeds and raisins from the cabinet. Jessica added those ingredients, along with honey.

While Jessica stirred vigorously with a wooden spoon, Laura watched the "men." They were looking on with interest, their pitiful half-eaten sandwiches forgotten.

"Ready, Mrs. Laura!" Jessica reached for a table knife and proceeded to spread the lumpy mixture on slices of bread. Laura came behind, adding slices of banana and the second slice of bread, then cutting each sandwich on the diagonal.

Carefully Jessica placed the triangles on a plate and held them up for inspection. "Is this great or what?" she demanded.

Zach licked his lips. "Uhh…do I get one?" He put the sandwich in his hand down and shoved it across the counter.

"Sure." Jessica offered the plate. "But Daddy

won't want one," she added confidently. "He says, anything a woman can do, he can do—"

"Uhh—maybe you'd better forget some of the dumber things Daddy says," Matt suggested. "There are some things men do better and some things women do better—like making peanut butter sandwiches. So if you ladies don't mind sharing, I'm ready to concede this one to you."

Laughing, Jessica passed him the plate. Laura just wanted to throw her arms around him and hug him. They *were* getting somewhere, it seemed.

Now all she had to figure out was where—and this was the last full day they'd be spending here so she'd better make up her mind in a hurry.

"Well," Laura said with bright bravado, "the kids are safely tucked into bed and here we are, the last night of our vacation."

"Or the first night of the rest of our lives." Matt grinned at her rather whimsically. "I can't believe we've been here for five days."

"Me, either." She picked up the fire stick he'd given her that first night and poked at the smoldering embers of the campfire. "I can't believe how well everything's gone."

"Think so?"

That response startled her. "Don't you?"

He shrugged. "In a lot of ways, yes. The kids have had a ball."

He sounded so sad. Impulsively, she touched his arm. "You don't sound as if you've had much fun." That possibility hadn't occurred to her before.

"I did, as far as it went."

She squeezed his elbow. "What's that supposed to mean?"

"Think about it." Seated on the ground near the fire ring which had been built up considerably by the children, he slid around to face her where she perched on the log. "Laura, it's been all I could do to keep my hands off you."

"Matt—" She felt torn by this revelation and thought it must have shown in her tone.

His gaze captured hers. "I want to make love to you," he said simply. "I've wanted to make love to you ever since I saw you that first day you went to work for the *Review*. I thought I'd gotten over it after you slapped my face—"

She groaned. "I explained that."

He nodded. "And I've got no problem with your explanation. It's just that for the last couple of years, that was enough to let me convince myself that I really wasn't interested in you, anyway. Only I was lying. I am interested. Spending time here with you this week has made me want you even more, if that's possible."

His declaration made her tremble. She tried to draw in a deep breath but it stuck somewhere in the back of her throat. "I...I don't know what to say," she whispered.

"You could say you feel the same," he suggested hoarsely. "Or you could say I'm crazy and tell me to take a hike—never darken your door again. But I don't think you really want to do that."

Her mouth was so dry she could barely form words. "Y-you don't?"

"Nope." He touched her wrists lightly, then ran his hands up her bare arms to the elbow. "You've been so different this week—so free and easy. I think that's because you've decided I'm not so bad after all."

"I never thought you were bad, exactly. I just thought we couldn't get along on any sustained basis."

"This week has proven you wrong."

"Yes, but that's because of the kids. We've both been so busy trying to see to it that they have a good time—"

"Liar."

He touched her lips with his fingertips, damming the flow of words and sending a shaft of pure sensation rifling through her. He continued in the same tight voice.

"The kids are having a great time but all I'm doing is dreading the return to the real world. Will we also go back to the way things were between us?"

She caught his wrist between both of her hands and slid his fingers away from her mouth, down her cheek to her throat. "Things can never be the way they were before," she said, searching to the depths of her soul for honestly. "Too much has happened…too much is going to happen."

His eyes widened as if with sudden hope. "Laura, does this mean…?"

She sighed. "It means I want you, too, Matt. I—"

The rest was lost in the passion of his kiss. When

he rose to his feet and pulled her up to stand before him, she didn't protest because there was no protest left in her. When he bent to lift her into his arms, she sighed and let her head fall against his shoulder. This was meant to be, she thought foggily. Why had it taken her so long to understand that?

Only when he carried her into her bedroom, kicked the door closed behind them and deposited her on the bed, did she find the strength to act. And what she did was reach up to twine her arms around his neck and pull him, off balance, onto the bed with her.

At that moment she realized she never wanted to let him go because...because she loved him. At last she was ready to risk everything.

She woke up alone the next morning, but she woke up smiling. In the middle of the night, he'd held her close and whispered that he had to be back to his own bed when the children awakened. Otherwise, he'd murmured against the sensitive skin of her throat, nothing and nobody could have forced him from her bed.

She'd wanted to tell him then that she loved him, but shyness made her hold her tongue. There would be plenty of time for that later, when they were back in everyday surroundings and a declaration of love couldn't be put down to the emotions of the moment.

So she'd kissed him one more time and let him slip from her arms and disappear into the darkness. And then she'd lain there reveling in long-dormant feelings he'd somehow managed to awaken in her.

When she crawled out of bed she was singing. She

awakened the children with the kisses she longed to rain down on the face of the man lying in a bottom bunk grinning at her. The quilt draped around his waist revealed the broad smooth chest against which she'd rested her cheek, against which she'd pressed her lips so passionately.

"Pancakes for breakfast!" she announced. "Come on, sleepyheads, today's the day we pack up and head for home."

Jessica rubbed at her eyes with a fist. "But I don't wanna go home," she complained.

"Me, neither," Zach agreed. "I wanna stay here and fish some more."

Matt sat up, the quilt pooling lower. "Tell you what, sport, if we get everything done in time I'll take you fishing one last time. Is it a deal?"

"Deal!" Zach's eyes were shining.

Laura gave him a hug but she was watching Matt. "I love you," she said, ostensibly to the little boy but also, in her heart of hearts, to the man. "Last one up's an old maid!"

With much giggling and commotion, they leaped out of bed.

Matt and Zach were fishing while Laura and Jessica packed the last of the food when Dylan drove up. He opened the door of his pickup and a big furry beast jumped down.

"Fluffy!" Jessica rushed to hug her Siberian husky. "Thanks for bringing her, Uncle Dylan."

"No problem, kid." He grinned at Laura. "I

thought you folks could probably use some help packing up for the trip back down the hill.''

"That's a nice thought," she said, "but everything's just about taken care of."

"Yeah, I can see that." He cocked his head and looked at her, his expression calculating. "I guess everything went all right?"

Laura couldn't stop grinning. "Just great. We had a wonderful time."

"You look like you did. Uhh...where's Matt? I'd like to say hello before I leave again."

"He took Zach fishing. The creek is just—"

"I know," Dylan assured her. "I've been here before."

"Oh, of course, how silly of me." The bemused expression on his face was making her blush. "When you find them, just tell Matt I'm ready when he is."

"You know," Dylan said in a lazy drawl filled with nuance, "I'll just bet he'll be glad to hear that." Touching the brim of his cowboy hat with two fingers, he turned and sauntered down the path toward the creek.

The sight of Dylan swinging down the trail did not please Matt. Leaving the boy staring intently at a fishing line that refused to move, he rose and met his friend halfway.

"What are you doing here?" he demanded bluntly.

"I'm glad to see you, too," Dylan said agreeably. "I thought you might need help but I see you've got everything *well* under control."

Matt didn't like the man's tone. "Zach," he called,

"it's time for you to head back to the cabin with your fish. Tell your mama I'll be right along."

"Do I gotta?"

"Afraid so."

The small boy complied but he obviously wasn't happy about it. Matt waited until he'd passed Dylan on the trail before demanding, "What the hell's that supposed to mean, well in control?"

Dylan's shoulders rose in a shrug. "You know what that means. I've already seen the lady and she's happy as a lark so don't get testy on me now, my man."

Matt made an unintelligible growl. "I'll show you testy if you don't turn around and drive back down this mountain. You're not needed or wanted here."

"Calm down, Matt. I'm not bad-mouthing the lady. Hell, I like her. I'll be glad to go just as soon as we settle the bet."

"Screw the bet, Dylan. It was your little joke, not mine."

"It was no joke and I'm ready to pay up—if I lost, which I don't think I did." Dylan fished around in the pocket of his light denim jacket and pulled out a baseball, ragged and discolored with age. Tossing it in the air, he caught it with the same hand. "So what is it," he asked softly, "the lady or the baseball? Did you sleep with Laura or not?"

Matt had never thought it would come to this because he'd counted on having the strength to resist her. If he and Laura hadn't made love, it would be the simplest thing in the world to say so and send

Dylan on his way minus one priceless autographed baseball.

Only it hadn't happened that way and now Matt found himself in the unenviable position of having to lie to protect Laura, in which case Dylan would forfeit the prize, or tell the truth and betray her.

"I don't want your damned baseball," he growled. "Take it and shove it where the sun don't shine." His throat hurt with the effort to force out those words.

"Temper, temper." Dylan shook his head pityingly. "Look, Romeo, did you sleep with her or not? That was the bet. The fate of this priceless baseball depends on it—not to mention considerable cash."

"What cash?"

"I hate to break this to you but half the guys in Rawhide have laid bets on whether or not you've bedded the luscious Laura—now, don't take a swing at me!" Dylan dodged aside. "I didn't say anything. Everybody knows you came up here together."

"Dylan," Matt said in a deadly tone, "there are times I wish I'd drowned you that day when we were nine instead of saving your sorry butt."

"Sticks and stones," Dylan retorted. "All I want's the truth. Did you sleep with Laura or not—and remember, this is your best bud talkin'. If you lie, I'll know it. Trust me, I will."

"Okay, Dylan." Matt felt as if he'd been turned to stone but he forced himself to turn, to confront. He didn't like to lie but he'd do it to protect her. "I'll tell you the damned truth about me and Laura and then maybe you'll—"

Movement on the trail caught his attention and he stiffened, all the breath knocked out of him as if from a blow.

"Yes," Laura said in a tone as clear and cold as ice water, "tell him, Matt. *Tell him the truth!*"

CHAPTER TEN

"LAURA, wait!"

But she couldn't. Turning blindly, she rushed back up the trail toward the cabin. Exploding into the clearing, she saw Zach standing by the door looking lost and confused. Jessica was nowhere in sight.

She grabbed his hand and dragged him toward the Jeep all packed and waiting. "Come on, honey, we're going home."

"But where's Jessica? Where's—?"

"Never mind that, we've got to go *now!*"

"But—"

She lifted him into the back seat and fastened his seat belt with hands that trembled so badly they would barely function. All she could think about was the awful burning need to get out of here before she had to face Matt again.

For she would surely self-destruct if she didn't have time and space to pull herself together. He'd made a fool out of her and she'd not only let him do it, she'd helped him. Well, he'd got what he was after. As far as she was concerned, she never again wanted to lay eyes on that…that…

Fighting tears, she drove the Jeep over the dirt road, bouncing toward the sanctity of home and hearth. Never again, she repeated over and over; never again would she trust a man.

She was through with men for good this time.

She pulled into the driveway before her garage, killed the engine and with a sigh, laid her forehead against the wheel. This was all just a terrible nightmare, she prayed. She'd open her eyes and find—

"Mama, look!" Zach sounded greatly excited. "Look!"

Slowly she raised her head and forced herself to concentrate on the sight that met her eyes: her family room, all finished, just like the picture in her head— at least from the outside.

Of course, appearances often lied.

Zach unsnapped his seat belt and opened the door. "Can we go see?" he asked. "Can we?"

She followed him inside and to the new room into which she'd put so much time and effort and dreams and money. All she could think was, Matt had this done while we were gone so that when we got back he wouldn't have to see me again. It was all part of the setup...nothing *but* a setup.

Zach giggled with delight. "It's just bee-oo-tiful," he announced.

And it was. Everything was exactly as Laura had envisioned it. Despite Matt's dire warnings about all the changes she'd insisted upon, the end result was perfect. It was so perfect that she couldn't stand to look at it any longer.

Maybe she never would. What had he done, ruined her pleasure in her new family room at the same time he was ruining her life?

*   *   *

The minute Jessica got home, she snuck away from her father and called Grandpa's newspaper. "May I speak to Katy Andrews?" she asked in her most grown-up voice.

"Katy Andrews here."

"Aunt Katy, it's me, Jessica!"

"Hi, honey. I thought you were still at your grandpa's cabin."

"I just got home."

"Why are you whispering? I can hardly hear you."

"I don't want Daddy to know I'm calling. Aunt Katy, you said you'd help me."

"Help you do what?"

"Get Daddy and Mrs. Laura together. I need help—lots of help. Zach will help but he's just a little kid."

After a long pause, Katy said, "Something bad happened, huh?"

Jessica nodded violently, realized that didn't work over a telephone line and said a heartfelt, "Yes! Will you help me?"

"Of course, but I'm not sure what I can do. Tell you what, I'll be finished here in another fifteen minutes or so. Why don't I pick you up and we'll go have a soda and talk this over."

"Oh, Aunt Katy, thank you! I knew I could count on you."

"Yeah," Katy muttered. "I just hope your faith isn't misplaced."

After Katy drove away with Jessica, Matt sat on a stool at the breakfast bar and tried to decide what to do next. Laura was angry, all right, and he really didn't blame her. But was he willing to walk through hot coals to convince her?

Hell, yes! He picked up the telephone receiver and dialed her number. The machine came on. "Laura, this is Matt. I've got to talk to you. Please pick up."

She didn't.

He dialed in again. "Laura, I apologize for everything. Everybody deserves a second chance. Pick up the damned phone and I'll explain everything!"

She didn't.

Matt paced around his sunny kitchen, scowling at the instrument of torture. Grabbing it again, he called her for a third time. "Laura, you're being childish. You can't avoid me forever so why not spare us both a lot of grief and pick up the phone!"

She didn't.

Maybe she was out. That possibility, slim though it might be, buoyed his spirits considerably. They stayed buoyed through the next half dozen calls. After that, they plummeted.

He felt stupid going to her house and pounding on her door but desperate times called for desperate measures. He felt even more stupid when Roger Reedy, the city planner, pulled over to the curb and called out through an open car window.

"Anything wrong here?"

Matt, shoulders hunched, ambled over to the car. "Nah, everything's just great," he said sarcastically.

"That's good." Roger rummaged through a stack of envelopes on the seat beside him, extracting one triumphantly. "Here." He offered it to Matt. "This'll save me a stamp."

Matt examined the heavy square envelope. "What is it?"

"A wedding invitation."

"Who's getting—?" And then he knew. "You and Meredith Zink? Jeez, you barely know the woman!"

Roger laughed. "Like that matters," he said. "She's the one, all right. I knew it the minute I saw her." He waved and began easing away from the curb. "You don't have to hit *me* over the head with a two-by-four!"

Matt, who did indeed feel as if he'd been hit over the head by a two-by-four, stared after the silver sedan. Some guys had all the luck.

And the rest of us make our *own* luck. He'd have to think this over and come up with some plan to repair relations with the woman his ex-friend Dylan called "the luscious Laura."

Laura spent Saturday unpacking and doing laundry, in between Matt's attempts to breach her defenses. He left messages on her telephone; she wouldn't pick up or call him back. He banged on her door and called her name; she hid in the bathroom with the water running.

In between she tried to figure out why she continued to feel so lousy. She'd known what Matt was and what he was after from the beginning. Snap out of it! she commanded herself. This, too, shall pass.

Only it didn't.

By the time her boss called Sunday morning, she

was just as miserable as she'd been driving down the mountain. She picked up reluctantly, supposing he was going to ask about the vacation—or worse, would already know what had transpired.

He surprised her. "Hate to land on you when you're not due back at work until tomorrow but we're in a bind here," he said without preamble. "Your fill-in had a family emergency yesterday and I've got nobody to cover the annual city ice cream social."

"That's today?" Drat.

"Yep. I know you'll want it for your Monday page, especially since I hear the mayor and the city manager are going to hand out a bunch of joke awards."

Ah, the joys of small town journalism. "Can't Katy do it?"

"You know how she gets when I make her do anything that isn't straight news. Besides, she's already had a hard week."

"Then how about—"

"Laura, it's your page. Do what you think is right."

They chatted for a few more minutes about the goings on of the previous week but never once did he ask how her vacation had gone. Which could only mean he already knew and was too polite to rub it in.

Hanging up, she stood for a moment with her hand on the receiver, wondering what she should do.

As if she didn't already know. Laura Gilliam was nothing if not reliable. She'd go to the darned ice cream social, but only because she knew Zach would enjoy it, and because she knew there was little chance

of Matt showing up. He hadn't, in the three years
she'd attended.

He'd probably be out celebrating his "victory"
with his friends.

Gritting her teeth, she squared her shoulders. The
sooner everything got back to normal, the better.

"So how was the vacation?" Katy asked over a bowl
of freshly churned ice cream covered with mounds of
ruby-red strawberries.

The moment Laura had dreaded ever since she'd
arrived was at hand. "Don't ask," she said, stirring
her own ice cream into a molten mass.

Katy perked right up. "Uh-oh, what happened?"

"Nothing I'd care to talk about."

"Look, I'm not hanging around being your best
friend just so you can keep secrets. Give."

Laura sighed and looked away just in time to see
Zach run past with a pack of kids his own age. The
park bustled with civic pride; members of the city
council manned—or in the mayor's case, "woman-
ned"—the ice cream freezers and everyone was having a high old time.

Except Laura. She took a deep breath. "Katy, I was
right about him all along."

"I take it you mean Matt." Katy looked deadly
serious for a change.

Laura nodded. "I already knew what he was but I
let myself forget, just for a little while."

"There's always the chance you've misjudged
him."

"No, there isn't. I heard him admit it himself." *Did*

you sleep with Laura or not? Dylan had asked. And Matt had replied, *Okay, you want the truth, I'll give you the damned truth—*

By now, every man in town would know that Laura had slept with Matt—they'd laid bets on it, for heaven's sake.

"No," she said again, "I didn't misjudge him. And I don't want to talk about him anymore. *Ever.*"

"But—"

"Not ever!" Laura picked up her purse and rose from the wooden picnic table. "Look, I've got work to do. I have to talk to the mayor, find out what the program's going to be about."

"Laura, I think this is probably all a big misunderstanding between you and Matt. If you'd just—"

"Which part of 'not ever' don't you understand, Katy?" With a wave, Laura turned away. At least there wasn't much chance of running into him today, she reassured herself. But when the inevitable finally happened, all he'd get from her was a cold shoulder.

"Daddy, please!"

"Forget it, Jess." Matt picked up the television guide and flipped through the pages—not that he was interested in television but he had to do something or he'd go nuts. His assaults on Laura's door and telephone had gotten him nowhere, until he'd finally admitted that he was wasting his time.

"But I want to go to the ice cream social!" Jessica almost stamped her foot in frustration, apparently remembering just in time that would only make her father mad at her. "Everyone will be there," she whined.

"Not everyone. *We* won't."

"You're mean." A couple of tears rolled down her cheeks. "First you do something awful to Mrs. Laura—"

"I certainly did not!" He stared at her, horrified: his own daughter!

"Then why is she mad at you?"

"How do you know she is?"

"Com' on, Daddy." She gave him one of those superior looks. "She won't talk to you on the phone. She won't talk to you at all."

"Maybe so, but why does that mean *I* did something wrong? Did it ever occur to you that she might be the one in the wrong this time?"

Jessica considered. "No."

"Well, that's just great," Matt snarled. "My own kid."

Jessica began to cry in earnest. "That's why I want you to apologize to Mrs. Laura, Daddy. Then you can go ahead and get married, so me 'n' Zach can have a real family—like, one mother and one father, one boy and one girl, one cat and one dog. Is that too much to ask? *Is that too much to ask?*"

He pulled her into his arms and hugged her, thinking that it wasn't too much to ask at all, but it wasn't going to happen with this particular woman. "Honey," he said, calm again, "Laura and Zach won't even be at the ice cream social. She's still on vacation until tomorrow."

"You don't want to see her?" Jessica sobbed.

"I…" Suddenly aware of what he was about to say, he stood her away from him so he could look into her face. "I don't think I should be discussing my love life with my nine-year-old daughter," he said with a tight grin. "Okay, you win. We'll go to the ice cream social, but don't say I didn't warn you."

She held back. "But if Mrs. Laura *is* there, you'll apologize?"

"Yeah, sure." But she wouldn't be there.

"And then you'll get down on bended knee and ask for her hand in marriage?"

Matt laughed. "Sugar, you read too many fairy tales. Prince Charming, I ain't, your famous newspaper ad aside. Now go wash your face with cold water and we'll go see what's cookin' at the park."

Jessica skipped to do his bidding. Boy, she thought, is he in for a surprise!

"—and then we're going to finish up by issuing a challenge from the planning department for a tug-of-war with the building department—Laura, are you listening?" Mayor Marilyn leaned around and got right in Laura's face. "You look like you've seen a ghost, girl."

The bottom had dropped out of Laura's stomach, for she did indeed feel as if she'd seen a ghost—or a ghost's daughter. Jessica stood on the edge of the sidewalk leading from the parking lot, looking around anxiously.

Laura pulled herself together. "I'm sorry, Marilyn. Did you say a tug-of—?"

"Mrs. Laura!"

Jessica spotted her and came galloping over. She threw her arms around Laura's waist and hung on tight. Without a moment's hesitation, Laura hugged the girl back. Her father might be a jerk but Jessica was a lamb and Laura...loved her.

Marilyn beamed. "I meant to ask and just forgot—how was the vacation? But I guess this means it was just fine."

Laura shrugged noncommittally. "Jessica." She took the girl by the shoulders and moved her gently away. "Are you here alone?"

"Daddy's here someplace. Oh, Mrs. Laura, don't be mad at him! He's real sorry."

Laura swallowed hard. "Real sorry about what?"

Her suspicions were confirmed when Jessica said earnestly, "About everything."

Laura patted the girl's cheek. "This is nothing for you to worry about, Jessica. I'm not mad at *you*. We can still be friends."

"I don't need a friend," Jessica said desperately, "I need a *mother*. And I picked you, so what's the problem?"

Just then Zach ran up. "Jessica!" He slipped his arms around her waist and hugged her, pressing his face between her shoulder blades and his fists into her stomach. "I thought I'd *never* see you!"

"You're *choking* me," she complained, unwrapping his arms but slipping one of her own over his shoulder.

And both children stared at Laura as if waiting for something to happen. "Run along and play," she urged them. "I'm working here and don't have time—"

Her skittish glance brushed past a man, a man with broad shoulders and dark hair and a shocked expression on his face. Her first instinct was to run, but instead she lifted her chin and stared straight into his eyes before turning back to the mayor.

"And after the tug-of-war—"

Marilyn cut her off. "For heaven's sake, Laura, stop pretending there's nothing going on here. If Cinderella and Prince Charming had a fight, just remember how much fun it is to make up."

"This isn't something that *can* be made up." Laura poised pen over notebook. "So which contests will our mayor compete in? You're defending champion in the egg toss—"

"Laura."

She sensed his approach and was ready for the sound of his voice just behind her—at least, as ready as she'd ever be. "Go away, Matt," she said evenly. "I'm working."

"Won't you let me apologize?"

She whirled, losing her cool almost before she'd found it. "For what?" she snapped.

He stared at her. "For everything," he said as if that should cover all bases.

"That's not going to cut it, Matthew. Now if you'll kindly excuse me, I have work to do."

"Okay, tell me what you're so mad about and I'll apologize for that."

"You know what I'm mad about."

"Not really." He looked genuinely puzzled. "I

know Dylan said…'' He glanced at the two kids, at the mayor listening avidly, at Katy strolling up and trying to look casual about it—and failing. ''And I said… But I don't know how much you heard, so how can I be sure what set you off?''

''If you'd cared,'' she said coolly, ''you'd have come after me.''

''I did! I've been pounding on your door and dialing your number until my finger's about to drop off.''

''I mean, up *there!* You just let me drive home while you and your *friend*…'' Now it was her turn to remember their audience. ''…discussed the *gambling* habits of the men in this town.''

''Gambling?'' Marilyn demanded. ''Somebody's gambling in my town?''

Matt groaned. ''You heard that, did you?''

''Oh, yes,'' Laura said grimly. ''I heard that and plenty more.''

John came striding up. ''Marilyn, they're looking for you at the bandstand to—'' He stopped speaking abruptly. ''What's going on here?''

''Nothing,'' Laura said shortly. ''Zach, you run and play with the other kids while Mama does her work, okay?'' She turned to Marilyn, willing her voice to remain steady. ''I'll go along with you and see what—''

''Daddy, do something!''

Matt stared at Laura, his expression bleak. ''Jess, I think I've done just about all I can. Maybe it's time to admit defeat.''

"You do that," Laura said, her heart breaking. "Now if you'll all excuse me...."

And that was that, so why was she crying inside?

Jessica squeezed Katy's hand so hard the knuckles turned white. "What are we going to do now?" she demanded.

Katy looked thoughtful. "I'm not sure, but we've got to do *something*. What do you think, Zach?"

The little boy looked surprised to be consulted. He pursed his lips, thinking hard, and then he said, "Is this a chick thing?"

Katy laughed. "Yeah, I guess it is."

"Guys don't like chick things," Zach confided. "We like guy things."

Jessica frowned. "A chick thing." Her gaze met Katy's. "Are you thinking what I'm thinking?"

"I do believe I am."

"Did you bring everything?"

"Jessica, when you grow up, I'll bet you work for the Secret Service. You've got the sneakiest mind of any nine-year-old I *ever* knew."

"Thank you," Jessica said. "Zach, come with me. Aunt Katy, go round up Daddy and get him in the right mood."

"Shall we synchronize our watches?" Katy asked.

"I don't have a watch," Jessica said, unwilling to admit she also didn't know what "sinkernize" meant.

"Katy, have you seen Jessica? I want to blow this pop stand and the kid's disappeared."

"She's around here somewhere, Matt. What's your hurry?"

"Like you don't know."

"I don't, not really. All I know is that Laura's mad at you."

"I'm in her doghouse, all right." Matt rammed his fingers through his hair distractedly. "Not that it matters."

Katy jerked around to stare at him. "It only matters if you love her," she said softly. "If you don't..."

He just stood there, feeling as if someone had punched him in the solar plexus. If he loved her...would anything else matter?

"Laura!"

Startled, she glanced around instinctively. Matt stood there but it wasn't the indecisive and apologetic Matt she'd confronted earlier. Behind him lurked and loitered Jessica, Zach, Katy and John. The man looked like a Pied Piper!

"Yes?" she said coolly. "What is it?" She glanced at her watch. "I'm in kind of a hurry so..."

"I don't care how big a hurry you're in, I've got something to say to you."

"Yeah, Daddy!" Jessica pumped a fist in the air.

"Hush," he said. "This is my show. Laura, I want you to marry me."

"Ah, Daddy..." Jessica looked distressed. "That's not how you—"

"*Marry* you?" Laura thought she must have heard him wrong—either that or he was playing some horrible trick on her. "Of all the nerve!"

"Nerve? Damned right, it took a lot of nerve to ask you, the way you've been treating me."

"The way *I've* been treating *you?*" She shook her head in disbelief. "Matt, I heard what Dylan said to you about—about *you know.*" *About laying bets you'd get me into bed, about making a fool out of me,* she wanted to shout.

"So why didn't you hang around to see what divine retribution came to him after he said that?"

"Because I—"

Dylan emerged from a cluster of trees at that moment and Laura's thought was swallowed up by astonishment. He had the worst black eye she'd ever seen; all she could do was stare.

"Dylan!" she exclaimed. "What happened? You look as if you were hit by a train."

"A train named Matthew." He darted a pained look at his friend.

"Before or after he told you what a pushover I was?" she flung at him, her lower lip trembling.

"He told me he didn't get to first base with you and then he beat the—" He changed in midstream. "—the stuffing out of me for suggesting...well, suggesting otherwise."

Laura felt a little flutter of surprise, followed by hope she'd thought long gone. "He did?" She faced Matt. "Why?"

"Because," he said, "I love you, Laura. I guess I have for a long time but I didn't know it until..." He glanced at Katy. "...very recently."

Laura stared at him, at the children, at her friends,

and her head was spinning. "I...I...don't know what to say."

"Say you love me," Matt suggested. "You do, don't you?"

Jessica let out a peal of laughter. "Of course she loves you, Daddy! You're Prince Charming."

"Right now I don't feel any too charming," he admitted.

"You will," Jessica promised. "Zach, give Daddy the box."

Zach, who'd been watching wide-eyed, jerked upright and handed Matt the shoe box he'd been holding. "Here, Daddy!" he said.

Laura wanted to cry for all the jubilation in his tone, but she didn't have time to dwell on it. Matt was opening the box...staring inside...pulling out the biggest, most incredibly garish plastic shoe she'd ever seen.

"That's a glass slipper," Jessica explained, in case anyone missed the significance of the moment. "Isn't it beautiful?" She tugged on Katy's arm. "It's time!"

"Oh, yeah, right."

Katy reached behind her back and pulled out...something. Upon closer examination, Laura realized it had to be a magic wand: a flimsy paper plate cut into the shape of a star and taped to one end of a three-foot dowel which must previously have supported one of the signs pointing to the site of the festivities.

"Wave it!" Jessica ordered in an undertone that carried clearly.

Matt just stood there staring at the clear plastic

shoe, a perplexed expression on his face. Zach touched the heel reverently.

"Put it on Mama's foot," he said, trying to rush the proceedings. "I bet it fits just right!"

Matt looked at Laura and she met his gaze, her own eyes welling with tears. He took her hand and led her to a picnic bench where she sank down gratefully. Kneeling before her, he lifted her foot and slipped off her loafer.

"Will you marry me?" he asked softly.

"If the glass slipper fits…"

Slowly he guided her size seven foot into the size ten shoe, then looked up at her with his heart in his eyes.

She let out a little cry of astonishment and they all jumped as if they expected the worse. "My gosh," she exclaimed. "There must be a fairy godmother at work here—"

"Oops!" Katy waved the magic wand frantically, managing to hit Dylan on the side of the head. He grunted and sidled out of harm's way.

"—because," Laura sailed on, "this shoe fits me perfectly!"

And she threw her arms around the neck of her very own Prince Charming and whispered an unequivocal "Yes!" in his ear.

EPILOGUE

"I THINK we should a-lope," Jessica said. Success was within her grasp and she didn't want to risk losing it. "All in favor, say I!"

"I!" Grandpa said.

"I!" Zach waved his hand. "What's a-lope?"

"I heard Katy say it's when you run off and get married," Jessica reported.

Mrs. Laura's smile was beautiful. She looked really happy, sitting on Daddy's knee in her kitchen with his arm around her waist and the beautiful glass slippers kinda flapping on her feet. "Just a minute, you guys!" She tried to sound mean but she didn't fool Jessica. "Don't you think Prince Charming and I should have a say in all this?"

Jessica glanced at Grandpa for support but he shrugged and said, "Don't look at me! I already voted."

So Jessica looked at her daddy, who was kissing Mrs. Laura just behind the ear. "Whatever you want, honey," he said, and he wasn't talking to Jessica. "Just make it soon."

"On that," Mrs. Laura said, sounding out of breath like she'd been running only she hadn't, "we agree. But I don't think elopement is a viable alternative."

"Why not?"

"The kids— They'll want to be there."

Jessica was insulted. "I'm flower girl and Zach's the ring bear," she reminded them. Of *course,* they must be there. "And how about Grandpa? He wants to be there, too, right, Grandpa?"

"You bet your boots, little lady." He looked real determined. "I won't hold with any danged a-lopements."

"Then what shall we do?" Mrs. Laura turned to Daddy for guidance.

Daddy looked like one of those cartoon characters who get a bright idea and a light bulb goes off over their heads. "Your family room," he said. "Let's get married in your new family room. We're a family so what could be more appropriate? You don't have any furniture in there yet so we can rent chairs, borrow a punch bowl, call the preacher and just *do it.*"

"No, Daddy!" Jessica was horrified.

Daddy and Mrs. Laura looked at Jessica as if she'd gone crazy or something. "That's not enough," she said firmly. "Mrs. Laura has to get a be-oootiful white bride dress, and the flower girl gets to wear pink, and we've got to decorate and have lots and lots of flowers. Maybe Uncle Dylan can get us a horse and carriage like the real Cinderella, and Zach can wear short pants and carry the diamond ring—you *are* getting Mrs. Laura a great big diamond ring, right? That's what a Prince Charming would do, you know. And then maybe Mrs. Laura can—"

"Jessica," Mrs. Laura interrupted, "you sure do talk a lot. Come over here, honey. We need to get something straight." She wiggled her fingers.

Embarrassed, Jessica approached with dragging

steps. This wedding had to be just right. Nothing was more important, nothing!

Until Mrs. Laura said softly, "Call me mama, will you? It would make me very happy."

It made Jessica very happy, too, for that was when she knew for sure that she really had found the perfect wife for Prince Charming—and the perfect mother for herself.

MILLS & BOON®

Makes
any time
special

Enjoy a romantic novel from
Mills & Boon®

Presents...™   *Enchanted*™   *Temptation*®

Historical Romance™   *Medical Romance*™

MILLS & BOON®

Next Month's Romance Titles

♡

Each month you can choose from a wide variety of romance novels from Mills & Boon®. Below are the new titles to look out for next month from the Presents...™ and Enchanted™ series.

Presents...™

A BOSS IN A MILLION	Helen Brooks
HAVING LEO'S CHILD	Emma Darcy
THE BABY DEAL	Alison Kelly
THE SEDUCTION BUSINESS	Charlotte Lamb
THE WEDDING-NIGHT AFFAIR	Miranda Lee
REFORM OF THE PLAYBOY	Mary Lyons
MORE THAN A MISTRESS	Sandra Marton
THE MARRIAGE EXPERIMENT	Catherine Spencer

Enchanted™

TYCOON FOR HIRE	Lucy Gordon
MARRYING MR RIGHT	Carolyn Greene
THE WEDDING COUNTDOWN	Barbara Hannay
THE BOSS AND THE PLAIN JAYNE BRIDE	Heather MacAllister
THE RELUCTANT GROOM	Emma Richmond
READY, SET...BABY	Christie Ridgway
THE ONE-WEEK MARRIAGE	Renee Roszel
UNDERCOVER BABY	Rebecca Winters

On sale from 3rd September 1999

H1 9908

Available at most branches of WH Smith, Tesco, Asda, Martins, Borders, Easons, Volume One/James Thin and most good paperback bookshops

MILLS & BOON

MEDICAL ROMANCE™

HER PASSION FOR DR JONES by Lilian Darcy
Southshore - No.1 of 4

Dr Harry Jones is sure it's a mistake having Rebecca Irwin work
in the practice. Despite the raging attraction between her and
Harry, Rebecca fought her corner!

BACHELOR CURE by Marion Lennox
Bachelor Doctors

Dr Tessa Westcott burst into Mike Llewellyn's life like a red-
headed whirlwind. She said exactly what she thought, and
turned his ordered world upside down. It couldn't last. But
Mike had to admit, she lightened his life.

HOLDING THE BABY by Laura MacDonald

Lewis's sister was abroad and he was left holding the baby—
literally! He *badly* needed help with the three children and
asked Jo Henry to be nanny. In a family situation, Jo and Lewis
became *vividly* aware of each other...

SEVENTH DAUGHTER by Gill Sanderson

Specialist registrar Dr James Owen was everything Dr Delyth
Price ever wanted in a man. But Delyth had a gift not
everyone understood. James seemed prepared to listen, if not
to believe. Then she discovered his lighthearted side, and fell
even deeper into love...

Available from 3rd September 1999

*Available at most branches of WH Smith, Tesco, Asda,
Martins, Borders, Easons, Volume One/James Thin
and most good paperback bookshops*

Spoil yourself next month
with these four novels from

TEMPTATION.

MACKENZIE'S WOMAN by JoAnn Ross

Bachelor Auction

Kate Campbell had to persuade Alec Mackenzie to take part in a
charity bachelor auction. This rugged adventurer would have
women bidding millions for an hour of his time. Trouble was,
Alec wasn't really a bachelor. Though nobody knew it—he was
married to Kate!

A PRIVATE EYEFUL by Ruth Jean Dale

Hero for Hire

Nick Charles was a bodyguard on a vital assignment. But no one
had yet told him exactly what that assignment was! So he was
hanging around a luxury resort, waiting... Then along came
luscious Cory Leblanc and Nick just knew she was a prime
candidate—for *something*...

PRIVATE LESSONS by Julie Elizabeth Leto

Blaze

'Harley' turned up on Grant Riordan's doorstep and sent his
libido skyrocketing. Hired as the 'entertainment' for a bachelor
party, she was dressed like an exotic dancer but had the eyes of
an innocent. Unfortunately, after a little accident, she didn't
have a clue who she was...

SEDUCING SYDNEY by Kathy Marks

Plain-Jane Sydney Stone was feeling seriously out of place in a
glamorous Las Vegas hotel, when she received a mysterious
note arranging a date—for that night! She was sure the message
must have been delivered to the wrong woman. But maybe
she'd just go and find out...

Our hottest

TEMPTATION

authors bring you...

Blaze

**Three sizzling love stories available in
one volume in September 1999.**

Midnight Heat
JoAnn Ross

A Lark in the Dark
Heather MacAllister

Night Fire
Elda Minger

FREE!

4 Books
and a surprise gift!

We would like to take this opportunity to thank you for reading this Mills & Boon® book by offering you the chance to take FOUR more specially selected titles from the Enchanted™ series absolutely FREE! We're also making this offer to introduce you to the benefits of the Reader Service™—

- ★ FREE home delivery
- ★ FREE gifts and competitions
- ★ FREE monthly Newsletter
- ★ Books available before they're in the shops
- ★ Exclusive Reader Service discounts

Accepting these FREE books and gift places you under no obligation to buy; you may cancel at any time, even after receiving your free shipment. Simply complete your details below and return the entire page to the address below. *You don't even need a stamp!*

YES! Please send me 4 free Enchanted books and a surprise gift. I understand that unless you hear from me, I will receive 6 superb new titles every month for just £2.40 each, postage and packing free. I am under no obligation to purchase any books and may cancel my subscription at any time. The free books and gift will be mine to keep in any case.

N9EB

Ms/Mrs/Miss/Mr ....Initials...
BLOCK CAPITALS PLEASE

Surname...

Address..

....

....Postcode ....

Send this whole page to:
THE READER SERVICE, FREEPOST CN81, CROYDON, CR9 3WZ
(Eire readers please send coupon to: P.O. BOX 4546, KILCOCK, COUNTY KILDARE)

Offer not valid to current Reader Service subscribers to this series. We reserve the right to refuse an application and applicants must be aged 18 years or over. Only one application per household. Terms and prices subject to change without notice. Offer expires 29th February 2000. As a result of this application, you may receive further offers from Harlequin Mills & Boon and other carefully selected companies. If you would prefer not to share in this opportunity please write to The Data Manager at the address above.

Mills & Boon is a registered trademark owned by Harlequin Mills & Boon Limited.

Enchanted is being used as a trademark.

THE
Regency
COLLECTION

Where rogues find romance

Look out for the fifth volume in this limited collection of Regency Romances from Mills & Boon® in September.

Featuring:

My Lady Love
by Paula Marshall

and

Four in Hand
by Stephanie Laurens

Still only £4.99

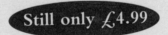

MILLS & BOON®

Makes any time special™

Available at most branches of WH Smith, Tesco, Martins, Borders, Easons, Volume One/James Thin and most good paperback bookshops